JOHN
the
REVELATOR

JOHN
the
REVELATOR

TJ BEITELMAN

Black Lawrence Press

Black Lawrence Press
www.blacklawrence.com

Executive Editor: Diane Goettel
Cover design: Pam Golafshar
Book design: Amy Freels

                    Black Lawrence Press
                    326 Bigham Street
                    Pittsburgh, PA 15211

Published 2014 by Black Lawrence Press
Printed in the United States

As this is a book in conversation with sacred texts and primary sources of various kinds, I have incorporated material from the publications below.

Excerpts from and references to *Down Singing River*, Emmett A. Betts and Carolyn M. Welch, eds., appear on pages 24–25, 67–68, and 99. From *BETTS BASIC READERS: THE LANGUAGE ARTS SERIES, Third Edition,* Down Singing River, by Emmett A. Betts and Carolyn M. Welch. Copyright © 1963 by American Book Company. All rights reserved. Reprinted by permission of Houghton Mifflin Harcourt Publishing Company.
All quotations attributed to individuals are taken from *Best Quotations for All Occasions*, Lewis C. Henry, ed.
Excerpts from the *U.S. Army Survival Manual (FM 21-76)*, Headquarters, Department of the Army, appear on pages 115, 214, and where noted in the text throughout pages 243–258.
All Bible passages are taken from the King James Version.
All word definitions are derived from *Webster's Revised Unabridged Dictionary* (G & C. Merriam Co., 1913, edited by Noah Porter).

For my father—

Contents

Acknowledgments

The germ of this narrative appeared as a short story of somewhat different form and focus in *New Orleans Review* under the title "Tiresias the Seer." Thank you to the editors for finding merit in it and, in so doing, encouraging me to ask the story, *What next?* For reading and responding to various early incarnations of the novel, I owe debts of gratitude to Robert Boswell, Rebecca Brown, and workshop groups at the Bread Loaf Writers' Conference and the Centrum Foundation, as well as to Katie McGriff, Keith Thomson, Laura Didyk, Anne-Wyman Black, and Iris Rinke-Hammer. Also, many thanks are due to Yvonne Garrett of Black Lawrence Press for her insightful editorial guidance in shepherding the book to completion. And, as always, thanks to Diane Goettel for her unwavering support of my work.

"…I have also used more personal pieces of friends and fathers. There have been some date changes, some characters brought together, and some facts have been expanded or polished to suit the truth of fiction."
—M. Ondaatje

"Other acknowledgements to friends are too deep and intensive to tabulate."
—J. Berger

Who's that writing? John the Revelator.
Who's that writing? John the Revelator.
Who's that writing? John the Revelator.
Wrote the Book of the Seven Seals.
—Traditional

I was not born in a one-room shack. I was not barred from any public school based on the dangers I posed to myself or others. I did not have to walk miles in the snow to the general store. No bears menaced me on the way. I did not stomp my feet, slap my hands together, and yell nonsense banshee yells to shoo the dark beasts off. I did not sing hallelujah come springtime and steal myself long draughts of cool creek water, sucking it straight from the clean babble like a fawn. There was not a gang of ruffians my age—or, if there was, they did not ride ponies through the woods, "a-hootin' and a-hollerin'." This demitasse gang that did not exist—not in this form, at any rate—likewise it did not come upon me in a summery clearing and ride in an ever-tightening circle around me. I could not feel the slight whirlwind it made; I did not hear—intuit—the hiss and rustle of frightened, fleeing snakes. The gang did not peel off one at a time, just as their animals could no longer manage the narrowing gyre, each boy laughing like the devil as I slumped to the ground. I did not gasp like a doomed, dry fish. I did not recall the incident for the rest of my natural born days.

And if ever I, as a mere boy, set out to walk across this Great Land with only a sharp knife and a busted compass that had no East;

    And if I then came to a great wide plain;

    And then, after that, a great wide river;

    And if, in time, I came to the very flat, very hot black mud of a delta where a buzzard befriended me, told me, Young man, that compass won't do, even I can see that;

And if I followed him as he flew in a slow slump eastward and eastward to a Swirling Place of Mad Green Thickets and Running Streams;

And if that great black Buzzard told me, Every prophet needs a home where they can hate him. Behold: you've found yours.

And if I then sat dumb in the cool water of a natural pool and watched that old hulk of a bird labor back into the westward sky;

If any of that had happened, I would have known from very near the beginning of everything that my life would include an inordinate share of magic and heartache. Miracles. Dark visions that only I could see. I would have known not to think I could cheat these essential circumstances. And, yes, I might have thought to finish it there, knowing—as I now do—that such a man as me can come to no good end.

But none of that happened.

Or if it did, I did not think to end it there.

I came to the end that was meant for me.

BOOKS OF THE LAW

History and Apocrypha

I

His sources:

—The ramshackle house where he once lived with his mother and father, far out in the green and vacant countryside, where not even a river would go. His mother still lived there—or he believed she did. He knew his father did not. He knew the man was dead in the ground.

The floor of the home was alive with vipers. Genuine vipers that ordinarily you might trip on in the woods. The ones with dry and dusty black backs. Outside was the decrepit shed. He could smell its thick must. At night, with the door shut, nowhere in the windowless world was blacker. Not even his wild-eyed father would think to look for him there.

—The back of Mrs. Beverly's English classroom in the seventh grade. Mrs. Beverly had an enormous behind and the thinly veiled bigotries of any self-respecting provincial school teacher. She was not bad or good. She was just what anybody might expect: her back to the class as she chalked up half-truths on the board: *I before E (except after C)*. He sat tucked in a corner of the very back row. From directly in front of him, Rebecca Cantrell's face presented itself in the pretty, puzzled scowl she so often aimed his way. The girl watched the black-haired boy hold his palm in the continuous flame of a plastic cigarette lighter. The sight or the smell or both caused Becky Cantrell to scream and scream and scream.

—Underneath the metal basin in the 6-x-9 cell at the Morris T. Duckworthy Juvenile Detention Center. They sent him there when he was thirteen years old, right after he took a thirty-ought and shot his mean father in the face.

The drip-after-drip of the faucet marking time.

The snakes are the stuff of later nightmares. All the rest is real.

II

The next-door bed pounded against the wall of his week-to-week room. A call and response. Moan. Yelp. Moan. Epithet. And rhythmic pounding (*headboard, wall*) to punctuate it. For the distraction, he made shapes with a stubby No. 2 on a blank page in a worn out composition book.

His default forms were these: house, fish, serpentine dead trees and rivers.

This was a habit his mother had started in him when he was very young, a way to ignore the noise around him, and he had kept it up through the many storms of noise that had passed through him. The silent white page a place to put the muddy river of his mind.

Of course, sometimes the outside world was too insistent.

This was one of those times.

He put the pencil down and closed the book.

It was almost ten o'clock, time to leave for the evening, so he walked to the sink. He ran the water and splashed his face and buried it in a towel. The amorous noises next door built and built.

"Nasty-ass people," he said to no one. His mother would have said they had lost their God-given shame, and she would have been right.

To drown out the sound, he turned on the television and sat at the foot of the bed. A bright new source of light. A cacophony of late local news, home-shopping, insignificant sporting contests, laugh tracks. Nothing. The young man switched off the television and sat there on the bed in the dark. Silence, then one loud crash from next door, then venomous cursing. The loud slam of a door. He went to the window. The bright fluorescence of the store dominated the street outside. The faint tinkling sound of a bell on the jamb echoed in the dark. A hunched-over figure emerged from the store banging a pack of cigarettes against its open palm. It coughed and spat on the shiny black road. This is the world he was going out into.

III

Outside the sky still roiled from a passing summer storm. Monster black-and-blue clouds sped past. A fat white moon peeked out at odd intervals. The town smelled like it always did: rubber on fire. The young man jogged across the street even though there was nothing coming that he needed to dodge. Nothing moved but the restless sky above him. His stomach grumbled—he had not eaten all day. It seemed the sound of it echoed forth, announcing his empty insides as something much larger and louder than what he showed the world.

IV

Inside was a wall of buzzing white light. Unrelenting. He squinted and pushed through it. It took him some time to get his bearings, but when he did, he made his way to the rotating wheel of brick-colored links. They were wrinkled up and thin. Sorry sustenance.

"Them dogs ain't no good, Boy Wonder," said the counter man. "They been under the lamp since four o' clock this afternoon." The man was fortyish, strapping, with small, mean eyes. His name tag announced him to the world as KARL.

The young man dug his fists into his pockets.

"And don't ask me to put no more on because I won't," said Karl. "Now's the time to eat anyhow. We got places to go and people to see."

Karl advanced on the franks and picked up a pair of tongs on his side of the counter. He tossed them one by one into the trash.

"Doesn't seem right," said the young man, "throwing food away."

"Since when did you get to be the authority on right from wrong?" asked Karl. "Somebody like you best stick with what little he knows."

Karl trashed the last dog from the rack. He flipped a switch, and the heat lamp went dark. He tied up the trash liner and plucked it from the bin in a giant heave.

"Almost time for me to close this shithole up. Go on out to the car. I'll be out in a minute."

The hungry young man eyed the trash bag. Plump with coffee grounds and cans and ashes and dried up wieners.

"I said,"—Karl's little eyes flashed their easy meanness—"get your sorry ass out of here while I close up shop. Christ Almighty, John-John. Don't you fucking hear neither? Ain't you but a fucking piece of work. I swear to God, it's a good thing you're halfway pretty."

Karl took him by the elbow like a disobedient little boy and ushered him out on his way to the alley with the dumpster in the back.

V

His life had always been a predicament, even before he had fallen in with Karl. When he was a boy, his mother would take him to the nearest town to buy their simple staples, mostly white rice and dry beans, sometimes a mess of wilted mustard greens. Though his clothes were ragged and he had smudges on his face, strangers sometimes confused him for a girl. It was the eyes—big and clear and questioning—and his hair: too often, no one had thought to cut it. It was also the curl of the boy's long lashes, which elicited genuine, envious coos from old women in the street.

News of the boy's mistaken identity unnerved his father. *That ain't right*, his father said. *It ought not to be that way.* He roughhoused his son, as if it would put more boy in him. He bumped him with his solid hip when they passed each other in the narrow hallway of the house. He boxed the boy's ears, pinched bruises into his sides, handed him a ball and made him run so he could chase him down and trip him up. The boy just got more timid. He hid or let his father pass with a wide berth. Soon his father's face reddened in his presence. One day the man said it again, once and for all. This time without any curiosity, without hope of a cure. This time as an infallible decree: *Something wrong. Ain't right. Ought not to be that way.*

———

Two versions of his birth:

The First

Feet first and reluctant. Days late. His mother moaned and the nurses took turns dabbing her face and neck with a cold, wet cloth. *This one's got other ideas,* they said. But biology betrayed him and out he came. He was nothing but elbows and useless friction on the way. Ten toes, two heels and knees, one nubby digit where his legs met. "How can he breathe?" his mother spat, pushing. "Why is he not smothered?" Had the masked man answered her, he would have said that her baby's lungs had learned a trick. They subsisted on her salty insides. This, a native language they would lose. But the doctor—a gaunt man whose prominent brow was all she could see from where she was—did not say a word. He held onto the ankles and tugged the boy out as if he was a dug-in tick.

The Second

They had taken his sobbing mother from the room. He sat as small as he could make himself, knees to chest, in the cramped, dark space. The smell of his mother all around him. Outside lay his father, faceless, sprawled across the bed. Tiny red shards of the man sprayed everywhere. At a distance, on the other side of the closet door, another man's voice cajoled the boy. It was a language of space and silence, distinct starts and stops, and it made him want to sleep there in the dark, forever, his finger still and always poised on the trigger of a gun too big for him.

While they likely misread his silence as unspent intention, he had none left. He waited for them to pull him from this dark, safe place. And they did. Feet first if not reluctant.

———

What he *could* do as a boy was swim. Underwater. He was a champion at holding his breath. There was a catfish farm not far from the broken-down house. He cut through the woods to get there, early in the morning or sometimes late at night. Times when it was wise to make himself scarce. As he got closer to one of the ponds, far from the big house at the front of the property, he jogged. His skinny legs ached by the time he got there. He slipped off his dirty clothes and his ragged shoes, and he submerged himself in the dark water. A catfish can grow as large as a man. He was not afraid. Even when he bumped into the heavy, whiskered things deep beneath the surface calm. He only wished that he had gills so he could stay down longer.

———

What else he loved as a boy was Sunday mornings. Most boys
did not love Sunday mornings, but he did. This was before his
mother stopped her church-going. She got up early, washed
herself, put her hair up in a bun. Then, for the one and only
time each week, she put on her face at the armoire by her bed.
The mirror chipped, cracked black from one corner to its
diagonal opposite. Some other family's heirloom swiped off a
heap headed for the junkyard. Her son sat on the corner of the
bed and watched her as her husband—his father—slept off his
Saturday night. When John was very young, it startled him to
see how easily she made an art of it. Her steady and deft hand
outlining her thin pink lips. A brush of fine, filmy powder on
her forehead, her cheeks, her long, straight nose, her chin.
The careful lining of the eyes. Her face was square and weary
but it had been pretty when she was younger, and the cosmetics
made her look more alive. Once, near the end of his life, her
husband rolled over in her direction, squinting against the
light. *Don't know why you take the trouble to do all that for church. Makes you
look whorish.* She glanced at her son and then down at her own
lap. *And you,* he told his boy, *don't be looking at your mama that way.*
Ain't *right. Get on outside. I'm trying to sleep.* He never saw his mother
put her face on after that.

———

A hot afternoon on a Sunday, inching down the hall and to the room. Willing the floor to be something besides an uneven instrument of creaks. All the boy's weight propped on the balls of his feet. The ache in both arches. That he carried all his fear in his slim shoulders. What he was afraid of:

Any number of discoveries—

That someone would find him in the room and at what point would this someone find him: standing timid and expectant before the armoire; running a finger along its chipped edge and then slipping both hands underneath the lid—this the point of no return.

And which of them would find him. His mother, whose privacies and privations he was rooting in. That her face would flash fear—this was sure. Fear of him and for him. The proportions of each would depend on whether he had any of it on his own face. He had not decided either way when he slipped into the room. A mask of faint colors anyone could find in almost any sky. Still—with or without the pastel smudges on his smooth face—she could make nothing but mistakes in what she thought it meant.

That he could make such a puzzle for her: that's what there was to scare *her*.

His father would know it for what it was: an act of war.

———

He was a boy who knew nothing of archaeology, but he knew in the way humans have always known that to dig into something is an act of intimacy. An intimacy no one can predict. To bury something is to forget it. To hide something and lock it away is to save it for yourself. A plain woman's tints and rouges. The means to change the way light interacts with the topography of a face. But more than that. Under the heavy, mirrored lid of her secondhand armoire were the rare artifacts of some other—real or imagined—version of herself. And so: which was which, that was the question. Were they buried, dead and gone. Or was it a place of preservation, somewhere to keep it only for herself. Sealed off but still alive. He could not know until he opened the lid. Even then he might not know. This is what scared *him*.

He pulled the butter knife from his front pocket and jabbed it into the lock. It gave way with a quiet click. He fit his fingers into the slim crack and lifted.

What he had never seen up close was exactly how it was arranged. The mound of it surprised him. That there was no order to it. Just tubes and brushes and cotton swabs. A dense heap of tools in the art of making a woman's face. Now, staring back at him, what he saw was not a woman's face or a man's. His black hair, longish and unruly. His wide blue eyes and high cheeks. A strong jaw, an imperceptible nose. An enviable symmetry of features if the long crack in the mirrored surface had not split his face into two uneven shards. He selected a tube of lipstick, a shade lighter than red. The tear-shaped surface that touched her lips. He opened it and ran it along the fatty part of his thumb. He covered that small part of him. Lost in the shiny surface, he did not hear his father enter the room. The clatter of the belt unlatching in a singular gesture of violence.

Sacred Text

She got me this blue-lined book so I would not make my markings on the wall.

I will not make my markings on the wall.
I will not make my markings on the wall.
I will not make my markings on the wall.
I will not make my markings on the wall.
I will not make my markings on the wall.
I will not make my markings on the wall.
I will not make my markings on the wall.
I will not make my markings on the wall.
I will not make my markings on the wall.
I will not make my markings on the wall.
I will not make my markings on the wall.
I will not make my markings on the wall.
I will not make my markings on the wall.
I will not make my markings on the wall.
I will not make my markings on the wall.
I will not make my markings on the wall.
I will not make my markings on the wall.
I will not make my markings on the wall.

I will not make my markings on the wall.
I will not make my markings on the wall.
I will not make my markings on the wall.
I will not make my markings on the wall.
I will not make my markings on the wall.
I will not make my markings on the wall.
I will not make my markings on the wall.

[Fig. #1. Two still buzzards in a dead tree. Watching. There is a small black speck of a house on a distant hill. A clear black sky.]

It used to be that she read to me from the same dusty little brown book with a stamp in it from the county library. She bought it off the used heap for ten cents. Most every night she read to me from it. Then she stopped, said she was tired, told me it is time for me to do my own reading. There are stories and then there are questions at the end that you are supposed to answer. Sometimes they are about the story but sometimes they are about other things. The one I like in there is about the Talking Fish—how the man and his wife were poor and he could catch no fish until one day he did catch a fish, a magic talking fish, who granted wish after wish after wish: a house with a garden and then a bigger house until the greedy wife wished for some strange impossible thing—to be king—and so the fish took it all away. Which is what happens when you ask for things.

What Do You Think?   Fact and fantasy

Can It Be?

A man can catch a big fish.

No.

A fish can talk to a fisherman.

Yes.

A wife can wish for many things.

Yes yes yes.

A little house can turn into a big house.

No.

A woman can be a king.

I don't know. Yes.

[Fig. #2. A fish in a hat. The fish has legs.]

[Fig. #3. A king with fat red lips. Pink cheeks. Wide eyes and a mane of black hair. A black buzzard nursing at his breast.]

His Advancement

I

John's association with Karl started almost immediately after he had been released into the workaday world. A panel of authorities deemed him fit to shed his history, join the society of men. They cited the mitigating factors: that he had never committed a crime of any kind before, that he was the product of impossible circumstances.

Furthermore, John had been no trouble during his incarceration. He kept quiet—none of the guards had ever heard him say a dozen words in a string—and he had invariably done what he was told to do, including tending dutifully to his studies (such as they were). Thus, John was given a chance to make a new, clean life for himself. With almost nothing in his pockets, almost nothing in his stomach, and no steady means of filling either empty thing.

His first night as a free man, it rained. He had a small wad of bills in his sock—his institutional severance. He wanted it to last, so he took shelter under a bridge. Days he slept in the college library, with its untold tucked away places; nights he walked the streets. He lived hand-to-mouth until even his small stash of seed money was gone. Then he became a scavenging bird. He dove dumpsters, and that is where Karl found him one night behind the convenience store, jackknifed into the mouth of the trash bin.

"Let me guess," Karl said to him. He dropped the fat bag of refuse he carried and dug into his shirt pocket for a cigarette. "You in need of a cash flow."

John extricated himself, his mouth and both fists full of discarded food.

"Got any habits?" Karl asked him.

John swallowed and looked down at the food in his hands. He shook his head no.

Karl took a deep drag off his cigarette. The tip burned red. "Not for now anyway," said Karl. "Come over here. Let's get you in the light."

He pulled John into a pool of streetlight, moved his smooth face in either direction to get a better look. Then he circled the young man. A cloud of smoke twirled around him.

"Yes, you'll do real well."

"What will I do well?" asked John.

"Favors," said Karl. "Come with me."

Karl whisked his new charge away in a 1978 orange Ford Pinto. The car rumbled, unmuffled, out to the truck stop at the interstate and sidled up to a purring semi. Thus began their entrepreneurial arrangement.

"It's a simple transaction," Karl told him. "Old as forever. You've got something he wants. He's got something you want. You're both willing to trade what you've got for what you want."

"How am I supposed to know what to do?"

"Don't worry about that. He'll make his preference known. Most important thing is payment's due *before* services are rendered. Period. That part's what I'm here for. You leave that to me."

John hesitated.

"You got another way to get thirty dollars for ten minutes' work, you go right on and do it."

And that was the calculus that sent him up into the cab. The man that night was wiry. He smelled like cigarettes and sweat. One look at John and his stone face became a sly smile. The wiry man retired to the back of the cab, and John sat there for a full minute, then part of another.

"Dammit, Nancy. I ain't got all night."

Men slept nearby in mammoth machines. Karl waited below, sipping malt liquor from a forty ounce bottle. A few hundred yards from where John sat, the highway ran to points far away. John up in this small, hot place facing a simple transaction, old as forever. His stomach growled. He breathed deep and removed his glasses. He took great care in resting them on the dash and then made his way back into the cab.

II

The truth was John did know what to do. The Morris T. Duckworthy Juvenile Detention Center housed up to 518 adolescent
boys and young men at any given time. Many of them violent,
all of them obsessed with finding novel places to put their gen-
italia. Or not so novel places. John was young for Duckworthy,
small for his age, and his features were fine. He did not last
through his first communal shower. Two older boys took turns,
one holding him while the other asserted himself. Over time,
he learned that if he did or did not do certain things during
the act itself, he could make it somewhat easier on himself.
Soon he could leave his body when it happened, float up to the
ceiling and watch it from a distance, like someone who studied
the peculiar habits of animals in the wild: *In certain species, young
predatory males seek out their weaker peers and impose upon them to engage in
homosexual acts—*

The human animal is nothing if not an adaptable beast,
and in confinement John grew into himself. The scaffolding
of his bones expanded, filled by food he had rarely eaten in
the free world—beef, milk, eggs—and firmed up by a regular
work detail that caused him to use his body to bear any number of modest burdens. Scythe the weeds all along the edge of
the tall fence that caged them. Carry fifty-pound bundles of
laundered sheets and towels. Use a hoe to turn the earth in the
ever-slumping garden that was meant to teach them to care
for something other than themselves. At the end of his time at
Duckworthy, John was still slim and not quite tall, but he was
not a child anymore. His body announced it.

His mind was something different, too. It was in Duck-worthy that his blurred vision was noted, documented, and corrected. The thick horn-rimmed frames a government issue. Until he put them on he had not known how sharp-edged all things could be. Each leaf on the far-off trees a separate ser-rated thing. The intricate hollows and swellings of a face. The delicate inland ridges of an ear. Everything more solid and knowable. Everything more real.

He took to the sad library because it was always empty and it no longer hurt his head to read. It was not, in fact, a library at all. It was a small room off the common room, near the shower. Long white bulbs strobed on and off from the ceiling lamps. More off than on. The room an empty afterthought. Gray. Dim. No sentry for the books jammed tight in waist-high metal bookcases. No one watched them because they were no commodity—it is not stealing if no one cares to know where the disappeared thing has gone to. What he loved most was the brittle paper. How careful he had to be with it. Like each page was a delicate, impossible life. Each page a body. Thin and dry and ready to break. Moths kissing his fingers. John took the unnecessary habit of lifting books, to read them in his bed at night. One at a time, shoved into his waistband. These he smuggled back, a careful, shuffling walk across the com-mon area—a no man's land—and into the concrete 6-x-9. This stealth let him think he shared a secret with another thing, these books his confidantes. These books, the places where he stole away. The nearly sacred places where he hid himself.

III

John stumbled down out of the rig quicker than he expected. The wiry man had been wired to explode. John's knees buckled when he hit the ground and the smell of diesel fuel swarmed. His mouth and throat felt filmy. He braced against the hood of Karl's Pinto and heaved up what little there was in his stomach. Mostly yellow acid. At this Karl winced. The fat, brown bottle made a hollow pop as he took it from his lips.

"Don't get any on the car, son. Bile's hell on the finish."

John gathered himself and got in the car. He was a mess: snot-nosed; glasses skewed; sweat and stains down the front of him. He slumped in the seat.

"I'd tell you it gets better, but I don't like to lie," said Karl. He counted out John's small portion of the proceeds. "What those men are about is an abomination. I don't know how they live with themselves." He folded John's share three ways and held it out to him.

"Go on. Take it."

John did not raise his head but he took the cash.

"Now you're talking sense," said Karl. "Don't spend it all in one place."

Karl laughed at his own joke and took a last hit off the beer bottle. Then he put the car in gear and maneuvered the Pinto back out into the night.

———

Tired, spent people filled the booths in the all-night diner. A stratus cloud of blue cigarette smoke hovered beneath the low ceiling. The waitress was named Mandy; she was too old and bony and lined for such a name. She was as spent as the people she served. More so, then, by definition. Sad silence bounced off the walls.

John was engrossed in the plate of food Mandy brought him. A fat cheeseburger, medium-rare. A mound of onion rings. Lemon icebox pie. He shoved it into his mouth, mostly with his hands, and rinsed it down with a towering glass of milk. He had never been so hungry, before or since. Long afterwards, he would remember how good it all tasted, even—or especially—after the night's peculiar and distasteful difficulties. Karl smoked his cigarette, produced a flask and poured some of whatever it was into his black coffee.

"I'll bet you'd tell me a real sad story," said Karl.

John kept his head down and ate.

"Daddy beat you up. Maybe Momma, too," said Karl.

"My mother never hit me."

Karl kept on. "You turned early to some means of self-inflicted escape. Inebriation. Then crime. Incarceration. More crime. Now this. Am I right or am I right?"

John spoke with his mouth full, juice dribbling down his chin: "What happened back there, you're just as soiled in it as I am. More, I'd say."

"True," said Karl. "But now you got something in your belly to puke up. It's win-wins all around."

"I like girls," said John, "like anybody else."

"Nobody said you didn't," said Karl. "Business is business. Supply and demand."

Karl sipped his fortified coffee and John pushed his glasses back up the bridge of his delicate nose. Another man in some other situation might have shoved the plate away to make a point. But John was too hungry for principle, and the food tasted too good, so he went back to eating in great bites.

IV

At the end of his first night with Karl, John had money in his pocket and his stomach was full. Karl had set him up with a room in the weekly motel across the street from the convenience store. No doubt, John's fundamentals had changed. Karl, the rainmaker.

John ascended the stairs to his room.

"Tomorrow, Boy Wonder," Karl called up to him. "We'll take us another spin in the Batmobile. It ain't all mean truckers out by the interstate. I got some regulars for you. That's a whole 'nother ball of yarn. Trust me now, I don't lie."

As the car drove out of earshot, John opened the door and entered his room. Amorous sounds from the room next door bleated out into the evening.

That night the dreams started in earnest. Of course, there was the one of the ramshackle den of vipers. That one was predictable. At intervals, the vipers would do different things: curse him (*You won't amount to nothing!*) or copulate or rise up and spit gobs of real venom at him. Sometimes his mother was there, sitting in her chair like she did, worrying her hands together and asking had he seen Daddy yet. Only a few times in these early dreams did he see Daddy, and that was the faceless version he had seen just after the point-blank blast. These vipers-in-the-homestead dreams always left him exhausted and trembling.

But there were other dreams, too. Those of his boyhood days: popcorn smells in warm gymnasiums in the wintertime; steamy pastures in the summer; musky, viscous catfish ponds; the lot behind the tractor shop where the boys pitched pennies. Things that had happened and things that had not, but pleasant things all the same. More often than not, these dreams left him feeling free and easy. As if he was not who he was, had not lived the damaged life he had lived thus far. When he put his head to the pillow in those, his first few adult nights in a week-to-week room, these were the dreams he wished for, these dreams that gave him hope for a restful sleep, if not some peaceful far-off future.

And then there were dreams of the far-off future. Peace was not a part of it. These were haunted, jumbled visions. It would be some time before he could remember them when he woke up, much less know all the things they were trying to tell him. It was not long before he took to writing them down in his blank book, to save for some as yet unknown posterity.

V

More often than not there was pocket money, and his days were free. John had lived worse lives than this. He could sleep through the morning hours, wake up with a long hot shower, no one sneaking peaks over at him. He could traipse through town, eat when and where and however much he wanted. If it got too hot—and it always did—he could retreat into the frigid library at the college, with its infinite stacks and its tucked away places to read or take a nap. If he got too bored or chilled, he could thaw himself on the steps and pass time watching the pretty co-eds jog around the quad. Usually he did not get bored. He read. Because he was not a student and could not check out any books, he rekindled his habit of lifting them. He found a first-floor window and tossed them into a bush below, then he would dig them out on his way back to his room.

When night fell, it was time to get ready for his rounds with Karl. It was a steadfast rule that he must be clean, so he headed back just before sunset so he would have time to wash the day off of him. Another long shower, then he always brushed his teeth with vigor. He brushed his tongue too. Karl told him about that. How it freshens the mouth. This he did with such force and depth that he often gagged. One or two rinse-and-spits. Then he would stare at himself in the mirror. Watery-eyed. Primed and ready as he could be for the business at hand.

His early days with Karl brought him into contact with a steady stream of miserable men possessed of weird, outsized desires. Some of these desires were stranger and larger than others.

There was the fat hairy man who wore a bustier and make-up and expected to be called Desiree.

There was the clean-cut handsome lawyer—a pillar of the community—who insisted John meet him late at night in his office. He sat behind his big desk, long legs crossed in an elegant scissor. He sipped scotch and talked about baseball for the greater majority of his allotted time before attending to the transaction. They did not touch each other. John was to take off his shirt and caress his own bare chest as the other man watched and took care of the matter on his own.

Then there was sad Melvin. John had to hold him in his arms for a solid hour, both of them fully clothed, as he kissed him on the bare forehead at regular intervals.

Less common were the standing engagements. Professor H was one of those. Wednesday nights and sometimes Sundays, too. The professor occupied one of the garden-style apartments adjacent to the college campus, where he spent his days teaching "the marginally talented youth of our time about the odd longstanding history of man." Professor H was a short, thin man with wavy silver hair. He smelled like gin and baby powder, and his apartment was immaculate. Persian rugs and antiques. Doilies. Like an old maid lived there. All of this had the strange effect of making John feel safe, like he had been there many times before.

The professor invariably set to spinning a record when John arrived. Billie Holiday. Nina Simone. Sad, slow music with bite in it. Sometimes he asked John to dance with him. Always he asked him to take off his spectacles.

"I don't care if you can't see a lick. Those are gems planted in your head, dear boy," said Professor H. "By Providence Itself. Show them off."

His apartment was, of course, laden with books. Burdened with them. Fancy books. Heavy books. Wide books. Flimsy little fancy books. In the milling around afterwards, waiting for Karl to return, John liked to scan the spines. One night, he felt the urge to snatch one off the shelves. He turned his back to the kitchen, where Professor H was pouring himself another glass of gin. It was a slim book—he didn't even read the title—and he thought he could stuff it into the front of his pants without the old man noticing. He reached for it.

"I'd offer you some, but I suspect you'll refuse."

Professor H lighted on the settee, ice tinkling in his glass. His little black dog, Edward, hopped up on his lap. They both grinned at John like they knew he was up to something.

"It's hard enough to keep my mind in order as it is," John said. He pulled his hand off the book and shoved his fists into his pockets.

"Yes, well," he said. "I believe a disordered mind is precisely the aim. So be it. Back to your browsing, then. It would not do for me, of all people, to dizzy a burgeoning mind."

John returned to scanning the spines. "I've never known someone to own so many books."

"Part and parcel of the trade, I suppose."

"I don't think I'd ever leave if I had so many. Not until I read them all. Have you read them all?"

"Certainly not," said Professor H. "This way I always have something to look forward to. You like books, then."

"Better than people."

Professor H sat in his underwear and slippers sipping his drink.

"Persons do have a tendency towards disorder. Whereas, in most cases, a book goes from front to back. You know what to expect. You can touch them, you know," he said. "They won't hurt you. I promise."

John picked the same slender volume off the shelf and opened it. He held it close to his face so he could read without his glasses on.

"'Whoever discovers the interpretations of these sayings will not taste death,'" said Professor H. He giggled and sipped. "What an absolutely *gorgeous* lie."

Another bird-like sip.

"So you have to tell me which book you picked. I'm dying to know."

John flipped the book over and read the cover: "*Best Quotations for All Occasions.*"

"Excellent. Read me some. I'll tell you if they're true or not."

"'Behind an able man there are always other able men,'" he read.

"Not always, no. Unfortunately. But then that's where a lovely young fellow such as yourself comes in."

"'Facts are stubborn things,'" read John.

"God, yes," said Professor H. "Stubborn and ugly and crass. I prefer a pretty lie any day, don't you?"

"Is that how college professors talk, in riddles?"

"That's how I talk. You're certainly not the first person to be put off by it."

"I'm not put off."

"Thank you. You're sweet to pretend."

Just then, a car horn honked. Karl. Without saying anything, Professor H got up and went over to the shelves. He was lighter on his feet than John had seen him before. He put his drink on the floor and squatted before the books, ready to search with both hands and all his concentration. He put on his reading glasses, which always hung around his neck. He plucked one book and then another and then, after some time and with some growing frustration, he found several more. He handed them to his newest pupil just as Karl honked his horn again, this time louder, more insistent.

"These should at least start you off," he said. "There's more where that came from, of course. You know where to find me by now."

Karl was an impatient sort, so he honked again. Even louder, this time.

"For heaven's sake," whined Professor H. "Does the man not know that *civilized* people live here?" He patted his young consort on the shoulder, pecked him on the cheek, and sent him back into the hard world from whence he came.

Epistle

J—

*Three more for your perusal. Fat compendia, I am afraid. But necessary staples.
Yours to keep. You need not read them all at once; you have the rest of your life
with them. Savor it.*

A contextual gloss, if I may. I am tempted to leave the KJV *to its own devices,
but I fear that's asking for trouble. I include it for no less than seven reasons: 1) it is
a library unto itself; 2) the measure of any sacred text is its capacity for paradox and
contradiction ("Consistency is the hobgoblin of little minds." — Emerson); 3) there is
something important about putting the idea of God in one's own manner of speaking;
4) I am old fashioned; 5) when I was a very young boy, my aunts paid me a penny
for every book in it that I had I read. Including the apocrypha. That eighty cents has
long since been spent—on I can't even remember what—and I am sorry to say my
aunties' intentions were thwarted. Godfear did not take root in me, as such. I was
not as much afraid of God as I was puzzled by him. God was a thing that engendered
questions, not answers:* Where wast thou when I laid the foundations
of the earth? *Or* Who shut up the sea with doors, when it broke
forth, as if it had issued out of the womb? *And so forth. We are all of
us so many Jobs—self-indulgent and ignorant sons and daughters of everything that
predates us. All we have is questions answered with more questions; 6) I am enamored*

of prophets, all shapes and sizes. A prophet may disobey all the rules of the rational world (and is, in fact, encouraged to do so), he sees into the hearts of men, comes and goes as he pleases, and so forth. For these enviable privileges, he must only prepare for the inevitable: one day, the rational world will burn him, stone him, or nail him to a cross. Or at least banish him to the woods, real or imagined, to leave him all by his lonesome. How small a price for knowing all our secrets; 7) most important: it has such pretty words ("For the waters of Nimrim shall be desolate: for the hay is withered away, the grass faileth, there is no green thing." Isaiah 15:6).

Yes, I believe that about covers it.

Which leads me to the Webster's*. There are tales—surely apocryphal to some extent—of illiterate prisoners who learn to read and write using the dictionary because that is all they have. At the end of it they are learned and erudite men with not only an unerring command of the language but of the whole universe of ideas at their disposal: history, philosophy, religion, science, and so forth. Yours is already a graceful, able mind, so I offer it not so much as a generalized course of study—though it could be that—but as proof that a word is a malleable thing that can grow and decay and even die over time. In the beginning was the Word, yes, but that Word is not always what it used to be. Words, like people, change. They adapt to their surroundings. If, that is, they want to survive.*

So, then, we come to the Army survival guide, which I admit is something of an attempt at humor. All three of these are a means of survival in their own right, of course, so there is something serious about it in the end: striking out and surviving on your own in the world is both a literal and a figurative exercise. (And if nothing else, one can entertain himself for quite a while just looking at all the diagrams and pictures).

Next time I hope we can start our discussion of A Tale of Two Cities*. Madame Defarge is delicious. I don't have it in me to think of her as a villain. But don't let me spoil it for you. Until then—*

Yours,

H—

Visiting Himself Upon the World

I

Early mornings were Karl's busiest periods. Tending to the coffee pots and the frozen drink machine, counting the drawer, checking the unisex restroom for filth that would not be ignored for one more day. This morning was singularly dreadful. A fidgety line of people waited to get in. The syrup and the ice in the frozen drink machine would not mix right, and the toilet had no water in it. He slapped out-of-order signs on both and opened the door to the flood of people. He was already in a foul mood when John walked in.

The line from outside had reformed itself at register. One or two people wore a blue uniform and a nametag, scrubbed up and ready for the day. Then there were others whose immediate prospects were even worse than Karl's, which was saying something. Numbered among the latter was a man with a patchy four-day growth and a red t-shirt that declared I AM MISTER CLEAN. He stepped up to take his turn in line.

"Marlboro Reds," he said. Karl noticed that both his front pockets bulged. Sure enough, Mister Clean rooted into them and pulled up two fistfuls of small change. Karl and the others in line let out an audible groan in unison, but Mister Clean was impervious and kept up with his diligent counting. When he got to the last coin, the young man stopped and his face fell. He searched his pockets and there he scrounged up three more pennies to add to the pile. His face announced a mixture of triumph and sheepishness.

Karl stared him down and slowly took one more penny from the Have-a-Penny-Leave-a-Penny stash next to the register. He added it to Mister Clean's pile.

"I see you plainly can't afford a slow death," said Karl. "River-drowning's a helluva lot cheaper. You ought to at least consider it." Then he reached up for the pack of cigarettes and tossed it onto the counter.

An embarrassed and muttering Mister Clean took his hard-earned Marlboro Reds and left. John passed him on his way into the store but he paid the scruffy man no mind. He made a beeline to the register, cutting in front of the next person in line, a pregnant woman buying a six-pack and two freezer-burned fudge pops.

"I was next," said the pregnant woman.

"I'm not buying anything," he said. Then he turned to Karl. "I need your keys."

Karl was already fit to be tied. He chewed his lip and breathed deep. "I'm working."

"Not hardly," said the pregnant woman. If he had looked at her, he might have punched her in the mouth, so he didn't look at her.

"Plus," he said, "I ain't gonna give you my keys. What kind of stupid do you make me out to be?"

"I just want to put my bag in there, not have to carry it around all day. It's heavy. I've got a lot of things in there. I'll bring you the keys right back."

"Why not just leave it in your room then?"

"It's just," said John, "easier this way."

Karl squinted as if he was thinking very hard, contemplating some deep matter. Life and Death. The Cosmos. He spoke in slow, measured terms.

"You wait your turn," he said. "I'll get these folks rung up and then we'll talk."

The line grew by two more blank-faced patrons.

"It won't take long," said John. "I'll bring them right back."

The pregnant woman stamped her foot and waived her ten dollars. "I was next. My ice cream is melting."

Karl plastered a smile on his face that did not do much to mask his contempt for everyone and everything in his midst. He addressed the entire stagnant line.

"If you'll excuse me, I have to deal with my associate. Won't be but a minute."

And he stormed out from behind the register, not even bothering to wait for John to follow him out the door. John took his leave, too, and that left the four or five of them clinging to the inconsequential provisions they had chosen to fuel the first few hours of their day. They grumbled and made their slow dispersal. The pregnant woman left her fudge pops and beer at the counter, but before she got out the door, she had another idea. When she was sure Karl was gone, she circled back around to grab her loot, shuffling out of the store, free and easy.

II

Karl was careful to avoid John's face. That would be bad for business. The beating was relentless all the same. Karl's indiscriminate right boot thudded into John's ribs and arms and legs. It seemed to go on forever, and while it did, John had occasion to split off from the moment, even from his own body. He studied, for instance, the underside of the Pinto. How much like a soot-black set of entrails it was. That thought sutured itself to another place and time. An earlier version of himself, seven or eight years old, hiding on a hot day underneath the rusted out pick-up in the yard. His father stomping around, pounding the sides of the truck, raging in an indecipherable tongue. The man's thick, strong hand digging in after him. Then the menacing poke of a broomstick. After that, the groan of the driver's side door, a few moments of cunning silence, then the strained sounds of his father's labor at the back end of the truck. Soon enough, John's temporary shelter had been pushed away, rolling harmless down the gentle slope of the yard. Nothing between him and the beating his father intended for him.

A boot to the kidneys brought him back to the alley behind the store. Karl was shouting down at him, kicking at points of emphasis.

"You are one sorely mistaken piece of shit. You think I don't know see the way you been here lately? Like you got it on your mind to take an adventure and leave poor old Karl behind. Last thing you need is anybody's car keys. That's a sure way to get yourself into more trouble than you know what to do with."

Karl exhausted himself and rested against the Pinto. He summoned a gob of phlegm from the depths of his chest and spat into the dumpster. John lay in a pulpy heap.

"Another thing," said Karl. He lit a cigarette. "This ain't no equal partnership. Hear? I make the fucking decisions. You just show the fuck up and do what I say."

Karl wrested the backpack from John, who did not fight him. He unzipped the pack and pulled out one thick text from a stack of them.

He pulled out the Bible like it was a severed head. "I seen it all now." He dropped it back into the bag and opened the hatchback.

"Ol' JC did run around with whores and no 'counts," said Karl. He slung the pack in, and slammed the hatch shut. "That didn't turn out too good for him, though. Guess that means I best be careful, huh?" He pulled the last drag off his cigarette and tossed it in John's direction. It bounced off his chest and smoldered near his face.

"You want that shit back, you may just get it but only if you play your cards right. I know where to find you."

When John was alone, he rolled over onto his back and stared up at the blue-gray sky. Everything at the center of him ached. His chest heaved.

He took his time to get up. At first he kneeled on one wobbly knee. When he got to his feet, he held his stomach like he had been gut-shot. He swayed in the still, trashy air next to the dumpster. The prospect of a long, sweaty walk to the library was too much. Instead he limped back to his room, closed the blinds, turned off all the lights. He pretended that the world and the rest of the day did not exist. Blinking in the dark, he came to some long-brewing conclusions:

Karl was not stupid. And he was mean.

John would need a better plan.

He could not do it by himself.

III

The blinds were drawn and the lights were off. Karl knocked at first and then he pounded.

"Open up. It's time."

John stepped out. He was clean. The evening breeze brought him a whiff of his own sweet, soapy smell.

"I'm ready," said John. "You don't have to be so damned loud."

John sat in the passenger seat and stared straight ahead. Karl drove and looked over now and again.

"Come on, now," said Karl. He grinned like a big brother.

John kept his mouth shut tight and leaned against the passenger's side door.

"What happened there this afternoon," said Karl, "that was just an assertion of the natural order of things. That's all. Best you learn it from me than from somebody else."

The street-lighted world outside crept past them, slow and self-assured and plastic, like a made-up thing, like a kiddie ride at the theme park.

"I took it easy on you," said Karl. No response. "Okay then. Take your time. You'll come around. Ain't no need to kill the golden goose."

That night was the same as it always was. Karl had two pre-arranged appointments and then it was out to the truck stop by the interstate. When it was through, they headed back toward town. Karl had a smirk on his face and a beer bottle wedged in between his thighs. John was spent. Long gone was the scrubbed sheen he had at the start of the night.

"You done real good tonight. That's what's called *professionalism*. There's hope for you yet."

"One more stop," said John. "I want to see the old man," said John. "He told me to come see him whenever. It just means more for you."

Karl gritted his teeth a little and the vein in his temple swelled. He took a swig of beer and steered the Pinto in the direction of the garden apartments over by the college. Not so much as a grunt out of him the whole rest of the way.

They drove through the neighborhood with its soft orange light and its canopy of trees. A train chugged on the tracks that dissected the neighborhood, and the sound served to calm John's mind. The Pinto glided to a halt in front of the courtyard. Some fraternity boys who lived across the street were on the porch drinking from plastic cups of beer, laughing deep and resonant.

John got out and was surprised to find Karl had too. Karl opened the hatchback and plucked out a package of something.

"Pick you up in ninety minutes," he said. "Don't you make me come in after you."

John went his way and Karl went the other. Just before he reached the door to Professor H's side of the building, John heard Karl's voice carry in the humid air.

"You boys look like you enjoy a good time. Am I right or am I right?"

John climbed the two steps into Professor H's side of the building and stood before apartment 2-B. He leaned his ear against the door. Cab Calloway leaked out. Minnie the Moocher. John felt his heartbeat in his throat. An insistent thud. Only the prospect of what was out there—Karl, the mischief he was making with the college boys—turned him back to the door and what he came to do.

He brought himself to knock and soon the door cracked open. Three little eyes poked out: one of the professor's and both of the little black dog's.

"Oh my lands," he said. "You poor dear, what has happened to you? You're carrying yourself like a waterlogged cat. Get in here this second."

Professor H hurried John down the hallway, into the living room light.

"Did they cut your tongue out too? Lord almighty, talk to me child. I'm not going to hurt you."

John pulled up his shirt to reveal his bruised midriff. Professor H let loose an aborted shriek.

"Who did that to you?"

"Karl and I had a disagreement earlier," said John

Professor H reached for John, who pulled away.

"I understand how you feel," said the old man. "But, dear boy, the last thing I want to do is hurt you. You just turn yourself back down that hallway. I'm going to draw you a nice bath. Bath salts and all."

The bathroom was as spotless as it was small. They had to orchestrate their movements, John disrobing and Professor H filling the clawfoot tub with warm, fragrant water. Bruises mottled John's trunk and limbs. The professor had to turn away from the sight and make his way out of the small space.

"That's going to make me cry, sure enough," said Professor H. "You soak in that tub. When you're ready, I'll make you a meal to stick to all those bones you've got showing."

Professor H stooped to gather John's dirty clothes.

"Take your time, sweetheart," he called over his shoulder on the way out of the bathroom. "There's a robe on the back of the door for when you come out."

John let himself slide down in the tub so that he was flat on his back with his head underwater. He opened his eyes to a warm blue blur. There was a low hum in his ears. He could hear his own heartbeat, easy and rhythmic. He turned his body and curled his legs up. All of him submerged. As safe and warm as he had ever been, seemed like. He stayed down in it as long as he could, until his empty lungs would no longer let him pretend he did not need air to breathe.

IV

Professor H stood over the stove wearing an apron. In one cast-iron skillet, he was frying three eggs in several thick pats of butter. In another, he was turning a slab of country ham. A small pot of grits simmered. There were biscuits in the oven. He took the ham off the heat and slid it onto a plate. Then he started working up a pan gravy with milk and flour.

When John came into the kitchen, his hair was combed straight back in a slick, black swath. He wore the satiny pink robe the professor had pointed out to him. It was too small and showed all his bones. He looked slight and waifish, but clean, and he no longer carried himself like a wounded animal. His arms were not crossed over his chest, his shoulders did not hunch. He stood there in the light and presented himself to his host.

"Don't you clean up nice," said Professor H, who motioned for John to sit at the table as he plated the eggs and grits and ham. He took the hot food with a glass of milk over to the table and put it in front of John.

John offered a quick nod of thanks but waited with his food before him.

"Eat up," said Professor H. "Breakfast food should be taken as hot as you can stand it."

"I don't have anything to eat it with," said John.

"Gracious, yes. It's been a long time since I've cooked for somebody," said Professor H. "Unless you count Edward, but I can't see how anyone could. His tastes are so indiscriminate. Not a damn thing he won't eat, I don't think."

Professor H retrieved a fork and a knife and a cloth napkin from the row of drawers by the stove. He made a show of folding the napkin and setting it to the left of John's plate. He did the same with the utensils

"Thank you for this," John said. "I didn't expect it."

"Nonsense," said Professor H. "Dig in. Don't let it get cold on you now."

John was hungry but he took pains to be as mannered as he knew how to be. He pulled the napkin out from under the fork and knife and put it in his lap. Taking up the utensils, he carved himself a small corner of ham and broke one of the yolks with it. The professor tended to what was left of the meal.

"Save room," he said. "There's more coming."

He finished up the gravy, pulled the hot biscuits out of the oven, and brought the second wave to John. On his way there, a loud buzz sounded and John flinched in his seat.

"Clothes are ready," said Professor H. "A nice bath and a meal and clean clothes, too. I think I missed my calling. I should've been somebody's grandmamma."

The old man giggled on his way to tend to the clothes dryer. He let his hand come to rest on John shoulder in a brief gesture of affection as he passed. John let him do it. He even let himself take some comfort in it.

After he ate, John sat in the armchair in the living room. He felt sluggish and full. There was music. Maybe it was a waltz or some other form John did not know. Something old and measured.

"This is the music of kings and queens," said John. He was heavy lidded and felt like he might fall asleep.

"In a manner of speaking," said the old man.

"Everything is jokes and riddles with you," said John.

"They are so-called 'defense mechanisms,'" said Professor H. "You're smart enough to know that by now."

He and his dog sat on the couch across from John, the professor with his feet up under him and the dog curled up against the place where the back cushion met the old man's hip. The dog locked eyes with John as if to ask him whether he was worth all this doting. As an answer, John came out with it.

"I didn't come to get a bath and eat breakfast," he said.

"You didn't? But that's what everybody does," said the professor. "People come from miles around. I'm famous throughout the county for my baths and breakfasts," He grinned at himself and sipped his ubiquitous gin drink.

"Maybe you are," said John. "But I came because I need your help with something. It's important."

"For you," said Professor H, "I'd give anything a try."

"What did I do to make you like me so much?"

Professor H put his drink on the coffee table and let out a conspicuous sigh. "I suspect a cynic might say it was for raw aesthetics. By that I mean you are a cute boy and I am an old man who very much likes cute boys."

John had hoped that was not the answer.

"But that is only the ugly, stubborn fact of the situation. There's more to it than that."

Professor H then sprang up and held out his index finger, signaling John to hold that thought and wait right where he was. As if John had anywhere else to go. The professor hustled back to the bedroom and returned with a rubber band pinched between his index finger and thumb.

"A little metaphor by way of a demonstration in the basic elements of potential energy," said Professor H. "If you will allow me: this is a common rubber band. Seen another way, however, it is the essential unsullied version of a sweet, kind soul called John. Now. What happens when you put this sweet, kind soul into the crucible of modern life?"

The professor pulled the rubber band back like a slingshot. Edward perked up.

"It stretches to the breaking point. All it wants to do is go back to its original state but it can't. Which seems like a very sad story. But it isn't. Do you know why?"

"I don't think so."

Professor H released the little band and it zipped all the way into the kitchen. Edward chased after it.

"Potential energy, my dear pupil, is the difference between where something is now and where it's going to be. The wider the gap, the greater the energy. That's what I like about you," said Professor H. "You've got more potential energy than you know what to do with."

"How do you know?" asked John.

"It's plain as day in those big, blue eyes."

Edward trotted back into the living room, the rubber band dangling from his little mouth. Professor H scooped him up and thanked him for the retrieval with a kiss on the head.

"I've confused you again."

"You're not as much of a puzzle as you think you are," said John, "I've been keeping up with my reading."

"And? What sense are you making of all that nonsense?"

"That it's time for me to go out on my own."

Professor H held up the rubber band: "Tomato, tomahto, seems to me."

"I tried before but all it got me was a beating," said John. "I need a plan."

"I would consider it my great privilege to be your accomplice," said Professor H.

"It means lying to Karl," said John. "Probably not much of a pretty lie at that."

"Don't underestimate me," said Professor H, "I've always longed to be an honest-to-God thespian."

And thus their conspiracy was born.

V

"That old man's took a shine to you."

They drove slow, windows down, as the night died. The apocalyptic smell of burning rubber enveloped the town.

"He likes my potential."

Karl almost choked on his guffaws.

VI

John emerged from his room at the appointed hour. The day was already starting to heat up. Regardless of what the next few minutes brought, he did not intend to return. His few belongings were still in his pack, which was buried in the back of Karl's car. Thus when he stepped across the threshold and onto the balcony he was empty handed. He shut the door behind him, and when he did someone stepped out of the room next door, where so many ruckuses of various sorts had emanated during his stay. John recognized her: the pregnant woman from the day before.

"You want a Fudgesicle or a Nutty Buddy this time?" she called back into the room. A pause. "I know you hear me." When it was clear there would be no answer, she followed her exasperated projectile sigh with the resounding gunshot-crack of a slammed door, stumbling a little from the force she had mustered. Her mound of a belly conspired against her equilibrium even under the best of circumstances. As she gathered herself, she noticed John.

"Take a picture," she said. "It lasts longer."

As she hurried past, John took solace in the fact that, even now, there were some lives for which he would not trade his own.

VII

The little man jogged into the store, a bright blur of color. There was a line at the counter but he whisked past, only slowing down to make eye contact with the clerk.

Professor H jerked his head in exaggerated motions toward the unisex restroom at the back of the store. Karl saw to the customers in line and then headed back to see what the old man wanted, quite certain that whatever it was would be a colossal imposition.

The restroom seemed even darker and dirtier than it was because it was too small for what little it housed: a grimy toilet and an even grimier sink, a condom machine on the wall that was perpetually empty. Professor H leaned lightly up against the sink, waiting with his arms crossed.

"What's got you bothered?"

"That boy you've been sending me is a mere child," he said. "Good gracious. What kind of person do you have me pegged for?"

"You really want me to answer that?" said Karl.

"Don't hurt my feelings. That's adding insult to injury."

"I do the best I can with what I can get. I've told you that before," said Karl. "Anyway, he thinks you like him special."

"I *do* like him special. Like a poor, lost stray. But what I'm looking for is some companionship. A quid pro quo of equals. Oh, it's just—" He sighed and cast his eyes heavenward.

"Out with it, chief. I got shit to do here," asked Karl.

"Smart man like you—I would've thought you had picked up on it by now. I don't know if I can even bring myself to say it."

"Then maybe you ought to keep it to yourself after all," said Karl. He fidgeted. His face formed his default mask of mean tension: brow furled; mouth a thin, hard line. "I'm just a go-between here. I can't be delving into your private affairs."

Professor H uncrossed his arms and he leaned in, slow and almost imperceptible, to reduce the thirty-six inch gap between them.

"I know that. It's just that if I had a preference, it would be for somebody . . . older. More savvy. Somebody with a bit of an edge."

Karl backed away but it was too late and the space was too tight. The old man lunged forward and latched onto him, running his hands over Karl's body, seeking out tucked away crevices, kissing his rough neck. Karl struggled at first to get a hold on him but once he did, he wrestled him into a compromised position against the sink. Arms twisted painfully behind his back. Face pressed hard into the faucet. Karl leaned into him from behind, with the force of most of his body weight.

"That's a-fucking 'nough," he shouted. Blood rushed to his face, and his voice was guttural. His spittle flecked the mirror. "You get a hold of yourself. You don't watch it, your steady stream of manlove dries up, but quick."

"You're hurting my arm." The professor clamped his eyes shut tight, as if this was all a bad dream in a fitful sleep. "Just let me go and I won't ever bother you again. This is all a terrible misunderstanding."

Karl tightened his hold, pressing the old man further into the sink. It produced a soft whimper.

"Ain't nothing to misunderstand. I ain't a fag and you are. That's all there is to it. Call me crazy but I don't want no queer old man groping me back here in the shitty ass bathroom."

"Of course," said Professor H. "You're right. How silly of me. My appetites got the better of me. Please. Karl. I'm not a young man."

"No you ain't, goddammit," said Karl. "You best remember that."

Then Karl jerked the professor up from the sink and pushed him out of the restroom.

John hid behind the dumpster in the alley behind the store. It had been a long time, too long for any fortunate outcome. He could feel what he had coming to him: the boot in the ribs, again and again, Karl's heavy stomp on the back of his legs. Then he saw the flash of garish color. Lavender and lime. Professor H's ascot was askew and his eyes were a little misty, but he was none the worse for wear. He sauntered up to the Pinto and John stepped from behind the dumpster. The old man tossed him the car keys.

"Henceforth I'm a bona fide pick-pocket," said Professor H. He got into the passenger side as John put the key into the ignition. "I must admit I found that rather intoxicating. Shouldn't we go burgle something?"

The Pinto grumbled to life.

VIII

"You were in here yesterday. Except you had fudge pops instead of Nutty Buddies."

The pregnant woman kept her eyes down in a vain attempt to go unnoticed. She looked for a second like she might run but she thought better of it.

"I don't think that was me," she said. She eyed the hot dog wheel with intent. Anything to keep Karl from looking her straight in the face. "I get that a lot, though. All pregnant women look alike, I guess. Plus I only ever eat Nutty Buddies. Reason being, a Fudgesicle is an inferior treat to a Nutty Buddy—"

A commotion outside interrupted her treatise on the subjective merits of this or that iced treat. An orange blur growled past the store. Karl was curious at first and then he checked the chain on his belt. In an instant, he was past rage. His exclamations were half-formed, equal parts lamentation and panicked plea to some Higher Power who held no sway over him under ordinary circumstances. Things could not be as they seemed. He jumped across the counter, pushed the pregnant woman out of the way, and bolted from the store. The pregnant woman wobbled a little then righted herself. She went to the door to see Karl sprint down the street after the Pinto, just to be sure he was not coming back any time soon. When he was out of sight, she returned to the counter to gather up her ice cream and beer, yet another gift from the Cosmos.

IX

They had driven around town for some time at Professor H's request, so that he could tell the tale of his daring deeds in intricate detail. Finally the Pinto stopped in the street in front of the professor's apartment building. He hopped out and poked his head back into the car.

"Are you going to be safe?" John asked. "He'll come for you. I can drop you somewhere while it blows over."

"I suspect he will come for me, and what would Edward do then? No sir. Don't worry about me. 'It is a far, far better thing that I do, than I have ever done.'"

John chewed his lip. "He said that right before he got his head chopped off," he said.

"Excellent reading retention," said the professor. "Clearly my work here is done. You be careful now. Suck the marrow out of life. And you know where to find me."

John turned the key in the ignition but the engine was already running so it let loose a screeching sound and stalled out. They winced together. John put the car in park and turned the key again, this time firing it up with its familiar, throaty rumble. He gave a wave, which Professor H returned with a mock salute, then he maneuvered the Pinto slowly down the street. The old man waved as the car proceeded for several blocks. The right blinker came on, quickly to be replaced by the left. The car slowed, stopped. It accelerated and made the left turn it had announced. A faint plume of black smoke escaped it, and then it disappeared.

TESTAMENT

I

Old Father Fish

"No other fish was as big as Old Father Fish.

No other fish had so long a tail.

No other fish was so old.

'Tell us a story,' said the little fish. 'Tell us how you
came to be so old.'

So Old Father Fish would tell this story.

When I was little, my mother would say,

'Play in the river

When you wish.

But stay away from people who fish.'

One day I saw a fly in the water.

'That fly looks good enough to eat,' I thought.

I rolled over on my tail. I looked again at the fly.

Then I saw a funny old man. He was fishing with
the fly!

'Oh!' I thought. 'My mother would say to stay away.'

So I did not eat the fly. I laughed at the man.

Then I thought, 'I must show this man how high I
can jump.'

I jumped and jumped, in and out of the water. At

last I made a very high jump, right into the boat. I could not get out!

'This is no place for me,' I thought. 'Why, oh why, did I jump so high?'

"The funny old man took me home. He called,
'My good woman,
Come and see.
Here is a fish
For you and me.'
His funny old wife came out. She looked at me and said,
'He's not very big,
But he will do.
Yes, he is big enough
For two.'

"Just then a blackbird came flying over the funny old house. When he saw me, he said,
'Why, I was just wishing
That I could go fishing.'
Down he came.
He took me by the tail, and we began to sail up, up, up!
Over the woods and over the fields we sailed!
Soon we were over the river. How I wished I were back in it!

Then I had a thought. I said to the blackbird,
'What are you going to do with me?'
The blackbird began to say,
'Why, I will eat you.'
But all he could say was, 'Why...'
That was enough. He let go of my tail.

"Down I went! Down, down, down, with the blackbird
coming after me! But he could not catch me. I was back
in the river with my friends. And here I have stayed from
that day to this."

[Fig. #32. A fish with its own white wings, a small black bird
in its mouth.]

A Consummation

I

The sun was high and the day was haze-gray with heat. The tires sucked to the road. In all his days John had never been this free, and he allowed himself to feel warm and good in those first few minutes on his own. He crossed the bridge over the brown river. A tug carried coal downstream, oblivious to the strange new circumstances of John's life. Soon he was past the edge of town, out into the green pastureland. Nobody and nothing around. He clicked on the radio because there was no one to tell him not to. Static and treacle-sweet melodies. He turned the radio off and tried to be invigorated by the wind from the open window, but the gentle up-and-down slopes and the unchanged scenery started to lull him.

On a long straight stretch of road, a few miles outside of town, he pulled the Pinto onto the shoulder and sat there in the silent, stifling heat. Green fields to either side of him. Maybe a house off in the distance. Not far from where he sat, a cow lay in the full heat of the sun, eyeing the alien orange thing in its midst. John felt as if he might have made a wrong turn somewhere, but he had made no turns at all. He only knew that he did not know where this road was going to take him or why he would want to be headed there. This was something new to understand about the life of a man free to do what he pleased: much of it is spent in transit from here to there, with no real *there* in mind.

That is when he remembered his stash of books. They were in his pack and his pack was in the hatchback, where Karl had slung it after their one-sided fight. He had nothing but time, so he took the key from the ignition and walked back to open the hatch. The cow still chewed and watched. John popped the lock and the hatch groaned open. There his pack sat. It was perched atop a problem he had not anticipated: a small mound of clear plastic bags stuffed full of cannabis. Karl's cannabis. Still another thing John had taken from him. He grabbed his pack but he kept his eyes on the pile of dope, as if it might somehow walk away. Because he had no one else to turn to, he turned to the cow.

The implacable animal kept chewing and it would not offer anything in the way of wisdom. John closed the hatch. He took off his shirt and wiped his chest and under his arms. There was not much he could do about it just then, and besides he was hungry, so he got in the car and tossed his soggy shirt in the passenger's seat. He fired up the engine and drove on in the direction he had been headed, fishtailing some as the tires made their way back onto the solid road.

The first prospect for provisions was an IGA store on the skirt of the next town. This was not a town per se. More the suggestion of a human residue. The IGA and one or two places like it to buy things. A smattering of small houses, a school. He wasn't yet far removed from the college town, not more than a dozen miles as the crow flies, but he'd found himself at the inner edge of the hinterlands.

He eased into a parking space in the IGA lot and checked his pockets. A single green and wrinkled dollar bill. He checked the glove compartment and the car's other nooks, half afraid of what else he might find. He found what he was looking for in the ashtray: a small silver pile of coins. He fished them out and headed in to see what it would yield.

On his way to the store, John passed a young woman who was leaning up against the wall by the Coke machine. She wore cut-off blue jeans and a tight white t-shirt. She was tall and slim and suntanned. A silver post pierced through two places in the top of her left ear, and she reached up to finger it as she locked in on this shirtless young man she had never seen before.

When he got to the automatic door, he saw the sign: NO SHIRT, NO SHOES, NO SERVICE. He turned back around to retrieve his shirt from the car, walking past the curious girl again.

"Hi," she said. "Nice pooper."

No one had talked to him this way before. Not a woman, anyway.

"I like your flat stomach, too," she said. "Where'd you get all those bruises?"

John did not answer right away. Instead he let his silence linger until he knew he had to fill it. "I like how brown you are," he said.

She laughed.

"Why is that so funny?"

"Because," she said, "that's a weird thing to say to a white girl."

She walked over to him. She was nearly the same height as him, so she could look him straight in the eye.

"I think you're going to spend the day with me," she said. And she took his hand.

"I have to get my shirt first," said John.

"Fine then. Let's get your shirt."

II

As he drove with the windows down, his left arm on the window in what had become his driving pose, his mind was spinning and his skin felt too small to contain him. He shoved his mouth full of Fig Newton. She sucked on an orange Nehi. They had pooled their resources to buy what they could, and Fig Newtons and Nehis was it. Her given name was Virginia. She leaned back in the passenger seat with her feet on the dash. She had found John's pack in the seat well, and dug through it like a curious child, picking out his KJV and flipping through the onionskin pages so fast she could only have been looking for pictures.

"That's a lot of words," she said.

"I like words," he said.

"Deeds not words," she said. "I haven't darkened a church door in a while, but I remember that's what our preacher used to say. All I know is words don't keep you warm at night."

She turned her attention from the Bible to his composition book. Here there were, in fact, pictures to go with the words, and she studied them.

"This your diary?" she said.

"I wouldn't call it that," he said. "But you can if you want to."

She found a line drawing of a buzzard. The caption beneath it read: *This is a black Buzzard. He brings the News.*

"You're one of those tortured souls in the back of the classroom, that writes poems and draws pictures and never says a word," she said.

"I wouldn't call it poetry."

"Well I can't understand it," said Virginia. "That probably means it's poetry. Most of those boys never get laid, you know. It's a good thing you turned out cute."

"So I'm told," said John.

"How come a real-life poet's got this plum ride?" she asked. "And how come he's all the way out here in the countryside?"

John kept his eyes on the road to not betray all the things he could be thinking.

"Uncle let me have it," he said. "Turns out I like to drive." Then he stuffed another whole Newton in his mouth.

"Careful," she said. "Don't choke on me. I've got to get you into some mischief first. A soul can't be properly tortured without having experienced its fair share of mischief."

John worked the Newton mush in his mouth and took a big swig of orange drink. The car sped down a barely paved two-lane road through the woods. There had been no turns or houses for some time. John undertook a deep consideration of Virginia's bare knee. She brought her hand over to scratch it, and he saw the faint, gossamer blond hairs on her arm. He felt the car list to the shoulder so he righted it.

"Where am I going?" he asked her.

Virginia tossed the notebook into the seat well in front of her and reached over to remove John's eyeglasses. She put them on her own face and giggled like it was funny.

"I don't know," she said. "Where *are* you going?"

"I can't see to drive," he said.

"Then don't drive."

She climbed into the backseat with John's coke-bottles still on her face. John kept driving through the blur. Soon her

shirt jettisoned into the front seat and landed in a ball in the
well. Then came her shorts. Then her underthings. John felt
his heart pound all the way out in his hands and his feet. He
squinted in the rearview and saw Virginia's smooth, brown
outline in repose. He chewed his lip, then allowed himself a
lopsided grin.

III

They found a shady spot, a tucked away dirt tributary off the main road. The day was as hot as it would get and the animals of the woods were making themselves scarce. Not even any birdsong. The only sound for what seemed like miles around was Virginia's unchecked, easy laughter. She lay on her back on the bench seat in the back, John's spectacles perched on her button nose. John, still clothed, lay on top of her, propped up on his elbows. His face inches from hers. She smelled so good it made him dizzy. He took the hornrims off her face and tossed them into the front seat somewhere.

"You have the prettiest eyes I think I've ever seen," said Virginia.

"You have the prettiest everything I've ever seen," said John.

"You are a poet, aren't you? But I thought you can't see without your glasses," she said.

"I'll come closer then."

He leaned down and kissed her bare shoulder. The faintest wave of goose bumps surfaced on the skin.

"That's the prettiest shoulder," he said.

Then he kissed her neck.

"And neck."

He kissed her ear and then her jaw line and then her nose.

"The prettiest ever?" she said. "All those places?" Now she was almost shy.

"That's what I'm saying," he said. He paused with his lips close to hers.

"Do I have the prettiest mouth?"

"One of them," he said.

"Shut up, you," she said. She pulled him to her. Their slow first kiss tasted good and sweet. Nehi and Newtons. John struggled to remove his sweaty t-shirt in the cramped back seat as Virginia fumbled to unfasten his jeans. All of that and what followed could not happen fast enough for either one of them.

A young man can be excused for the things in his mind leading up to the peak moment with a woman. Often it is what you would expect. A woman besides the woman he is with. Or he sees the woman he is with in some pose he feels sure she would not want to strike.

But sometimes the image that worms its way into his mind is not directly tied to the moment at all. Sometimes it is altogether random, disassociated. Maybe he recalls watching cumulus clouds in a high sky as he was supposed to be napping on his auntie's porch when he was four years old. Or it's the first time he got stitches, the doctor tugging the thick black thread through his tiny chin.

In this case, what came to John was not a memory, safe and self-contained. It was his faceless father, standing at a distance from the car, leaning up against a tree. The remains of his face curled into the rough facsimile of a smile. Like he was proud of his boy. John buried his own intact face in the pretty girl's hair and pressed himself as far into her as he could make himself go.

IV

The professor puttered around his kitchen, humming Liszt and wiping things down. For some reason he felt happy. Very happy. Happier than he had felt in a very long time. He put a kettle on for tea and headed into the living room. Edward slept, a small black ball snoring on the couch. The dog's little ribcage rose and fell. When Edward was a puppy, he was the runt of his litter. An ad in the paper had announced six mutt puppies free to good homes. Any homes at all, in fact, whether they were good or not. Edward was the last to go. A day or two from being stuffed in a sack and dumped in the river. The man who was giving the dogs away rooted him out from behind the lawn mower in the oil-stained shed. The dog's gums were white; fleas had almost sucked him dry. He had more worms in him than rightful insides. There was not a good reason that he lived, but he did. Professor H nursed him, sprinkled him with flea powder, fed him the white de-worming liquid through an eyedropper. Now there he was, alive, napping on the couch, which was now just one of a thousand things in the apartment that the dog claimed as rightfully his.

The professor was lost in this improbable affirmation of his own ability to nurture a living thing, so he flinched when Edward bolted up right where he was, stiff on all fours, barking with all the gravity he could muster. Just then a voice came from behind the professor.

"I guess you ain't the only sneaky one. Are you, Teach?"

Edward's protestations turned into a steady growl from deep in his throat. The professor wore a half-smile of resignation and modest bravery as Karl moved toward him. The tea kettle began its whistle. When Karl grabbed the slight old man by the nape of the neck, Edward went back to barking in earnest and the kettle whistled still louder. Karl started in and there would be no mercy or quarter, even though the man was old and weak and essentially good.

Vision

When I take the specs off I can't tell where I end and everything else starts. FOUR EYES. Which two are mine. When I was a boy I put my face close to the page to see the words I wrote there. All my world a foot or six inches away. Now that I see the full range of things I am meant to see I sometimes wish It would go back the other way. There is so little worth seeing, Here and Now or anywhere.

All the things I wish I could not see so clearly:

Offal on the shoulder of some faraway road.
Faces:
> *the hundreds of shapes a face can make that mean Pain or Doom or Never In A Million Years; then also how much like a child's a Pretty Woman's face can be.*

A crowded field of stars on any given night.
A burned-out shell, the black womb of a clawfoot tub.
I suppose most Everything Else.

[Fig. #39. A page of uniform blue-black ink pricked with a scattering of pinpoints where the white page shows through.]

Revelation

I

The Pinto sat parked at the lookout point of an enormous manmade lake surrounded by trees and rolling hills. A picture postcard of peace and serenity. A great hawk skimmed the surface of the lake, hunting the nimble, shimmery edibles just below the surface. Large houses dotted the edges of the water and the crests of the hills. The afternoon sun was soft and orange and low in the sky.

Virginia stared up at him, her head in his lap.

"Why'd we come here?" he asked.

"It's only my favorite place in the whole world is why," she said. She sat up and looked out at the water, as if to make sure it was still there.

"You know some rich man had all this built from scratch?" said Virginia. "They dug a big old hole and filled it up with water. Put houses all around it. Looks like it's been here forever, just like God planned it."

"I guess so," said John.

They both kept their eyes on the lake and did not say a word for a several long, strung together moments.

"You're too quiet," she said. "Tell me a secret."

"How do you know I have one to tell you?" he asked.

"You can't be a tortured soul without secrets. But have it your way. I'll go first," she said, her eyes still scanning the water, "Sometimes I think this place is the closest I'll get to heaven."

In the perfect afternoon light, she was even prettier than before. Sweeter. Less sure of herself.

"You seem like a nice person to me," he said. "Heaven likes nice people. Probably even better than people who make lakes that didn't used to be there."

Virginia lay back down with her head in John's lap. She took his right hand off the steering wheel and traced the lines of his palm.

"I have my moments," she said. "I'm just friendly by nature."

John let her trace his hand. Her face was intent as if what she was doing was serious business. It made him nervous because it made him want to hold her. He forced himself to look away from her, out at the lake, but that made him feel the light traces of her fingertips all the more. It was a fix, he was finding, to spend time in the company of a likeable woman.

"My husband says I'm too friendly sometimes," said Virginia.

John swallowed hard. Virginia kept right on.

"But most of the time I'm just making up for him because he's not very friendly at all."

She got up and searched around but there was no clock to read.

"He gets off at seven and I need to go meet him like I said I would."

John stared off into the distance and his jaw was clamped tight. The mask of someone not in the mood for any more secrets, his own or anyone else's.

"What?" said Virginia. "You look like you've seen a ghost."

II

Virginia had almost finished explaining the nature and origin of her relationship with Billy Ray. She met him in the waning days of her last year of high school. She had been visiting the Video & Tan in preparation for her senior prom. Her date was Garrett Tribble. They had gone steady and sexless most of the year and after the dance she intended to surprise him: no tan lines. On her third visit to the Video & Tan, Billy Ray was behind the register. He was tall and ten years older and she liked the way he called her "girl" even though he had never met her before. When he smiled, his face turned into a brand new thing. More alive than any single thing she had ever seen. She still went to the prom with Garrett Tribble, but it was Billy Ray who enjoyed her uniform brown glow afterwards.

"Probably it's because my daddy was a shit," she said. "Him being older and all. You'll like him. We can all be friends."

John kept quiet and drove. They sped down the State Road. It did not seem like he was listening to what Virginia said, but he was. With the Video & Tan in sight, he spoke up.

"It's a strange way to meet somebody. Already having taken liberties against him. Not really knowing you were taking liberties in the first place."

Virginia smacked him lightly on the knee. "Is *that* what you're worried about?" she asked. "That's nothing to fret over."

"I expect he might fret over it."

She rolled her eyes, as if this was the stupidest idea anybody could ever have. "Billy Ray is smart. *Real* smart. Either he knows what I do or he doesn't want to know. That's up to him."

She patted his knee again, this time with more affection, and leaned over into his personal space. She kissed him loudly on the cheek, to show how glad she was that it was all settled.

III

The Video & Tan sat just off the State Road, with a defunct batting cage in the next lot over and a grove a pecan trees beyond that. Sometimes a logging truck rumbled by. Otherwise it was just the road and the store and the high sky. An unlikely place for commerce.

A lanky man sat smoking a cigarette on the trunk of the one car in the lot. He wore aviator sunglasses and a clean black t-shirt tucked into crisp new blue jeans with a crease ironed into them. His dark hair was thick and combed straight back. The Pinto pulled into the lot, Virginia hanging out the passenger side window with a big smile on her face.

"Hey, Sugar!" she called. As soon as the car stopped, she jumped out. When she got to him, she ducked up under his arm and hugged him around his middle.

"Quit that fucker today," said Billy Ray. He did not hug her back. He did not even get down off the car.

"You did not," she said. She leaned back a little so that she could see his face.

"Said I would and I did," he said. "You know I don't lie about such things."

Virginia whooped and hugged him harder.

"That's my baby," she said. "About damn time, too. That Glenn's a bastard." She turned to the store and raised her voice. "You hear me in there? You're a bastard and I hope one of them rickety-ass tanning beds explodes and somebody sues your ass into kingdom come!"

Virginia stretched up on tiptoe and kissed Billy Ray hard on the cheek. Then she turned toward the Pinto to flash her proud smile at John, who had by then stepped out of the car to present himself.

"And just what did the cat drag in here, I wonder," said Billy Ray. He tamped out his butt on the trunk and tossed it to the ground.

"That's my new friend, John," said Virginia. "He's just the answer to all our prayers, is all."

Billy Ray grinned. "Makes me wonder what exactly you been praying for."

"Hush," she said. "We need a friend with a reliable mode of transportation. You know that, you said it yourself. Your mother ought not to have to cart us around, the shape she's in."

"Nothing wrong with Momma," said Billy Ray. "She just don't much like left turns."

Virginia rolled her eyes. "Right and straight ahead aren't her strong suits either," she said, mainly to John. "Not to mention stops."

"Girl," Billy Ray looked her up and down, "but aren't you full of piss and vinegar this evening." He turned his attention to the Pinto. He made a semi-circle of the vehicle, walked over to John and offered his hand.

They shook.

"Suppose it does save Momma a trip."

Virginia gave a little cheer and clapped her hands together.

"See," she told John. "I knew y'all would get along."

With that, she climbed into the cramped backseat. Billy Ray followed suit, but not before he paused to consider John one more time. He nodded as if to say, *All right then, here we are, let's see what happens now*, and then he ducked down and shoehorned himself into the too-small car. Once his two passengers were in the car, John made an accounting of his surroundings. The batting cage. The pecan trees. Glenn's Video & Tan. All of it in various stages of expiration. There was no other option. The State Road held out the only rough version of promise to be had. He climbed in and steered the car towards it.

IV

They did not speak because the wind whipped around them so loud and fresh it would have taken too much effort to be heard. A beautiful ruin of a landscape rushed by. They passed more pecan orchards, pastureland, and innumerable livestock. There were manmade catfish ponds and dilapidated family cemeteries. Martin houses dotted it all, here and there. With the recent clockwork run of thundershowers in the afternoons, the grass, the vines, the trees were all as green and full as they could be. The sun had already started to set red-orange over all of it, but in one corner of the sky yet another thundercloud approached.

They drove by a tall blue water tower. Then a one-stoplight town. Its bait shop, its church, its dollar store. Then nothing for a long time, then a fork in the road, then nothing but more cows and pasture until, at the bottom of a swale, there was a broad white sign in amongst a copse of trees a short distance from the road. Shady Manor Mobile Home Park.

"Slow up," Billy Ray shouted above the wind noise. "Turn in here."

The Pinto crawled over the long packed-dirt road that led into the trailer park. There was just the one route through the place with shabby mobile homes spaced out along the way. At the first trailer, they passed a lumpy old man who sat shirtless on the stoop. They passed a sunburned boy with no shoes pedaling his bicycle, a Frankenstein's monster of mix-and-match parts, no doubt snatched bit by bit off junk piles and grafted together over time. A mangy dog occupied the dead center of the road and took its time moving to let the car pass.

The park butted up against some train tracks, and just behind that was dense, dark woods. As the Pinto entered the sorry cul-de-sac closest to the tracks, a whistle sounded and a freight train chugged past in no hurry.

"Park it around back there," said Billy Ray. "Behind that yellow one."

John did as he was told and pulled the Pinto up on the grass, coming to rest behind a bile-yellow double-wide with an overgrown mess of bushes and weeds masking its false foundation. Out front lived a Mimosa tree in garish pink bloom.

They all got out and the one dark cloud in the sky opened up. It spat at them at first and then fat, round drops pounded the ground. The shower and the train and the dying orange sunlight made John feel like he was in one of his unreal dreams. His two passengers bolted up the stairs to the small, weatherworn deck attached to the back of the house. Billy Ray beat on the back door.

John would have followed them but as the train passed, he noticed a figure walking down the tracks in its wake. A darkskinned black man with fuzzy gray hair and a knotty old walking stick nearly as tall as he was. His gait was a nimble limp that suggested not so much his age but an in-born asymmetry somewhere in his legs, a condition he had long since learned to compensate for. He did not pay the rain any attention, no hunched over gait or quickened pace. When the man saw John, he gave a little hi-sign. John raised his hand in reply and pulled his shirt up to cover his head, then slowly made his way to the deck.

"Say the Devil's beating his wife," said the black man as he passed. "Ain't that what they say, Reverend Temple?"

Billy Ray pounded on the door again. "Yes, sir, Mr. Mose. That's what they say. You doing alright?"

"Raining soup," said Mose, "I'm out with a fork. Just like always. You tell The Man to come out and see me. I got some things ready for him."

"Yes, sir," said Billy Ray. "You stay dry now." Mose ducked into the woods and disappeared. Billy Ray went back to pounding. "Open her up, Momma. It's raining."

After a time, the latch turned and the back door opened. There stood Billy Ray's ratty-robed, mouth-breathing Momma. Her face and neck were a terrible maze of deep, haphazard lines. She was of indeterminate middle age, and her mouth was jammed full with bad teeth and the black-muscle tongue of a lizard. Her hair was a foul nest.

"You sure are a sight for sore eyes," said Billy Ray. He pecked her on the cheek on his way into the trailer, and she wiped it off as a mindless reflex.

"Guess what I did today. Quit that fucker, that's what I did. Hallelujah, praise God. That bastard Glenn just stood there with his slack-jaw wide open like he does. I said Glenn you better watch it or you'll catch some flies, boy! He didn't say nothing to that Momma because he couldn't say nothing at all. I had him."

Billy Ray's mother did not seem to care one way or another about the momentous news her son was sharing. Instead she glared out at her unbidden visitor. John took the steps one at a time and approached her with caution. When he got close enough, he offered his hand. The ugly woman pinched up her face and recoiled like he had instead presented her with a soft, steamy turd.

"Whoa now," said Billy Ray. He came back out to the threshold and wedged himself in between the two of them. "Momma's old school. Ain't right to reach for a lady, et cetera. Let her present her hand if she wants. This here's John, Momma. He's the one that give us the ride so you wouldn't have to."

He gave John's shoulder an encouraging couple of pats and went back into the trailer to renew his search for a beer. John was left to master the strange etiquette alone. As it happened, Momma did not choose to present her hand. She just eyed John and then retreated to the interior herself. John closed the door on the dwindling sun-shower and trailed behind her at a safe distance.

The Temple home was a low-ceilinged, utilitarian thing. The stale smell of fried fat and cigarettes clung to the walls and the soiled rug, the mismatched furnishings. A hallway led to two bedrooms, one for Momma and the other for Virginia and Billy Ray. A small kitchen opened out onto a living room that housed the barest of creature comforts: a recliner, a couch, a nineteen-inch television on a stack of crates.

His hosts had congregated in the kitchen. It was too small for the three of them, much less a fourth, so John hung back at the entranceway. Billy Ray was perched up on the counter sipping from a silver can. Virginia opened the refrigerator, fished out two cans, one for herself and the other she held out to John.

He shook his head. "I get dizzy," he said.

"That's what it's supposed to do, silly," she said. She popped it open and offered it to him again. This time he took it. She opened her own, clinked cans with him, and wiggled in between Billy Ray's legs.

"Devil's beating his wife out there, Momma. Raining when the sun's out."

"I think it's so pretty when it does that," said Virginia.

Momma dug through the pantry with a surgical intensity. She unearthed a box of sandwich cookies and took it with her to the recliner, leaving the younger folk to their own devices in the kitchen. She flipped on the television and leaned back into her own private oblivion, shoving cookie after cookie into her mouth. There was still no telling whether she could speak or not, though signs pointed to no.

"Not a damn thing pretty about it. Ain't that right Momma?" Billy Ray called out to the living room. No reply, unless unchecked munching counted for a reply. Billy Ray kept on, loudly so that his Momma could hear, as if she was inclined to listen. "Bad omen is what it is. But I can't worry about that because for once I'm in a good mood."

Billy Ray removed his sunglasses from their perch on the top of his head and hung them on his shirt collar. He downed the rest of his beer in a concerted flourish, then he maneuvered Virginia to the side and hopped down from the counter. All at once, and without warning, his face exploded into a snaggle-toothed grin and his eyes brightened. He put both hands on Virginia's face and kissed her on the lips. As she was stumbling back and collecting herself, Billy Ray strode up to John and did the same, only instead of kissing his mouth he planted one square on his forehead.

"Christ almighty," he said. "I'm happier than a pig in shit. This is the first day in the rest of my goddamn life, and not a moment too soon, either."

He bounded into the living room and stood behind the recliner. "I'd kiss you too, old girl, but I already done kissed you once just a minute ago, and I don't want to press my luck."

There were only cookies and the local news in her universe.

"What says the plan tonight, Momma? I think I'll call up old Chewie and see what mischief he can get us into."

Virginia tucked herself up under his arm. "Do we have to?"

"Do we have to? Shit yes we have to. This is a celebration, baby, and any celebration without what Chewie brings to the table ain't no kind of celebration at all."

She stuck out her lip in a pretty but affected pout.

"I don't know what Chewie brings to the table except piss-poor weed that don't do anything but give me a headache. Plus I can't understand a thing he says half the time."

"What am I always telling you about the Golden Rule?" said Billy Ray. "If you ain't got something nice to say, don't say nothing at all."

"That's not the Golden Rule," said Virginia. "The Golden Rule is do everybody else like you want them to do you."

"Same church, different pew."

Virginia talked right through him. "If I was a Mexican," she said, "peddling bad marijuana all across the county and saying crazy shit all the time, I'd have to expect that folks might get tired of it after a while."

"He ain't Mexican, he's Chinese," said Billy Ray. "Or whatever. And look here: Chewie's a nice young man and he means well. He's got some refining to do on his quality control, is all. He'd be the first to admit that. But I've always been one that don't like to throw the baby out with the bathwater. Anyway, John wants to meet him."

"John don't want to meet him," said Virginia.

"I think the young fellow can speak for himself. You can speak, can't you?"

"I can," said John, who had spirited into the room and sat in the far corner of the couch with his eyes on the television and his ear on the conversation. He was in the unfamiliar position of being the tiebreaker on a decision, albeit one of little consequence. He cleared his throat.

"I don't have much opinion on it either way," said John, "but I don't suppose I'd mind meeting your friend."

"Now somebody's talking sense," said Billy Ray. "So that settles it. I'll call Chewie."

"Fine then," said Virginia. She sat down on the other side of couch. "Call Chewie. I want to see what John says after he meets him anyway. I bet he don't like him any more than I do."

Billy Ray ignored her and went to the phone. "Momma," he said, "we are going to paint the town tonight, boy. Quit that fucker today, Momma. Just like I said I would. You'd a been so goddamn proud of your boy today."

His mother remained implacable, oblivious to the commotion around her. Up came the trace remnants of a sandwich cookie. She let out a toad-like belch, then went right back to stuffing her face.

V

A television's hold on a room is a powerful thing. After the call to Chewie had been made and that evening's festivities had been sketched out, the four of them settled in to stare at the glowing tube. Momma in the recliner, the other three sardined into the couch, two of them sipping full new beers and the other with his hands still folded around the one Virginia had opened for him.

On the news, the anchorwoman—a former beauty queen—closed the newscast with a great commotion about a man named Merriwether in Maycomb County who never left his trailer. The neighbors had not seen him in a decade or more. The only way they knew for sure he was still alive was that the mail kept going in and the refuse kept coming out. When he did die they found the place full of nothing but stacks and stacks of hundred-dollar bills. Hardly any room to move around. Many, many thousands of dollars.

Virginia was transfixed. "Wonder what he ate," she said.

"Hundred-dollar bills," said John.

She laughed bright-eyed, if a little tipsy.

"There you go," said Billy Ray. "Take a stab at some humor. We encourage that around here. You keep that up and we'll think you actually got a pulse."

Billy Ray pushed up off the couch and took Virginia by the hand. She trailed him into the kitchen, and they emerged with the rest of the six-pack. Billy Ray headed down the hallway with the beer and Virginia in tow. That was that. After a time, John heard Virginia laughing behind the closed door. He sat with the TV and the old woman. No use talking so he kept watching the television, now a mindless game show. What he mainly heard was a conspicuous silence now coming from the back. That and he heard the crunch-a-crunch of those sandwich cookies.

Free and easy life was turning out to be a relentless teacher. He had read in the quote book that *Everything changes but change*. The KJV offered a similar morsel: everything unto its own season. The survival guide said you must adapt to your surroundings to survive in this world. Eat what you have to eat when and wherever you can find it. It seemed to John that all of it went double for affairs of the heart. One short season with a lovely maiden in the backseat of a stolen vehicle. Another, hard on its heels, with her husband's ugly mother watching games of chance and/or skills of no consequence on the sad little television. Then again, he would come to learn all too soon that the lion's share of life as we know it boils down to just that: games of chance, skills of no consequence.

Exegesis

"New learnings are applied by the pupil during his silent reading and in activities following the silent and/or rereading."
—*The Betts Basic Reader*

It is like this. A faint star is easier to see when you do not see it straight ahead.
It is like people who chant their sacred prayers.
It is not like thinking. It is not like understanding. It is not like reading at all.
It is like knowing everything that has already happened and what is happening now and what will happen next.
All of this is a very big, impossible thing;

[Fig. 44. A string of tiny words formed into the shape of an ink black stream. At one place, the stream trickles out into a dust-dry bed of white.]

Starting in my fingers and ending in my toes. A twitch that tells me everything is about to change and that I have known it all along. I know a man is unhinged to say he knows what's next—for you, for him, for anyone. I know. *The old time prophets, major and minor, had hell to pay. I am less than minor. What I see is not the end of ends. I do not even see it. All I have done is felt it written as a faint echo inside my bones.*

[Fig. 45. A skeleton made of many dozens of bright blue imperfect eyes.]

Pilgrimage

I

"Can anybody explain to me why we can't go into town and get drunk like normal people?" said Virginia.

Billy Ray occupied the passenger's seat as John drove down the State Road. They were to meet Chewie at the ancient Indian mound village that was now haphazardly maintained by the state parks service.

"You're already drunk," said Billy Ray.

"I am not," said Virginia. "You're the one that's drunk."

Billy Ray nudged John with his elbow. "See now, that's how you know they're long gone. They get belligerent."

"Don't gang up on me," said Virginia. "Y'all aren't even friends."

"I rest my case," said Billy Ray.

Virginia let loose a groan. She sat in the backseat with one of her long legs stretched out in between the front buckets. The sundress she wore was pristine white and she, like her man, wore cowboy boots, except hers were brown and his were black. Her eye shadow sparkled and her lip gloss glistened. A plastic flower clip adorned her hair. A tipsy provincial angel, mumbling to herself in the backseat.

"Don't know why we can't just be like normal people."

Then she leaned her head against the window and dozed.

The Mounds were not far. Once they had been the seat of an ancient civilization, where great chieftain-priests lorded over robust markets—agribusiness, arms, energy—and the issues of the day. Healthcare and accessible medicines, the sorry state of public education, *what's wrong with kids today*. Etc. The Mounds were now not much more than a field trip destination for every fourth grader in the state. Here and there, in their ingenious little replica huts, lived a family of crash test dummies made up to look like indigenes. With their long, fibrous black wigs. And their soulless eyes. Also the parks service had erected a squat, ugly museum on the grounds and filled it with fish bones, broken peace pipes, pottery shards—the sorts of things people never intend to leave behind for posterity but always do—and a big, dug-out boat that once navigated the sluggish river bordering the property at the back.

Besides the park's public role as a stale history lesson, it had another function. More contemporary, less official. That is, it was a summer evening haven for all manner of nefarious aims. The flotsam and jetsam of the chief means of transcendence in the modern age—crushed beer cans, gooey prophylactics— littered the more secluded huts. *Look upon my works, ye mighty, and despair!*

Billy Ray had John pull the car into the deserted Dairy Freeze lot, half a mile away from the entrance to the park.

"We'll walk in from here," said Billy Ray. "No reason to draw undue attention to our little party."

"Everybody knows the cops around here go to bed at nine o' clock. Nobody else in their right mind wants to crash your party," said Virginia. "I'm staying right here."

"What if somebody makes off with you?" said Billy Ray. "Then where would I be?"

"I'd rather get my ass abducted than eaten up by mosquitoes and chiggers and whatever the hell else they got out there."

"You ain't much of a squaw then. Think of all the discomforts and hardships they had to reckon with. That and worse."

"And you can bet your sweet ass they bitched and moaned how miserable it was the whole damn time, too. No thanks. I'll stay."

"Suit yourself," he said. "I'll tell Chewie you said hi."

"Tell Chewie whatever you want." She spread out in the backseat, crossed her arms over chest, and closed her eyes. Almost like she was lying in state.

"You coming?" he asked John.

"Is she going to be alright by herself?" said John.

"I'll be fine," said Virginia. She didn't bother to open her eyes. "You better go and watch out for him. Somebody's got to. Chewie for damn sure ain't the one to do it."

Billy Ray, his face split into a wide grin, held a flashlight out to John. John took it and they were off.

II

With their flashlights off to conserve batteries and to go unseen, they trotted along the shoulder of the State Road. Once, a pick-up hurtled by and they ducked down into the roadside ditch. Then they were up again and advancing. On the way, Billy Ray spat reconnaissance at John: the dimensions and topography of the park, where the display huts were stationed, and so on. Billy Ray's pace quickened the closer they got to the entrance. John needed a half step extra to keep up with every one of his long strides. Soon enough, they stormed the main entrance and were at the mouth of it all, surveying the Mounds in their moonlit glory. Truth be told, there was not much to see—a half dozen sizable blobs of earth spaced out a few hundred yards apart. An understated if unmistakable geometry. The Mounds themselves rose no more than sixty feet in the air. Still, there was an aboriginal weight to the place.

"Every time I come here at night I get chillbumps," Billy Ray whispered, like they were in church.

"It's pretty out here," said John.

"It's fucking gorgeous," said Billy Ray. "And it scares the hell out of me all at the same time. You know what that means, don't you?"

John had felt that way around Virginia all day, especially when he touched her or she touched him. But he did not say that to Billy Ray. "No," he said. "What does it mean?"

"This place here is a portal to a Higher Plane," said Billy Ray. "That's exactly what that means."

Billy Ray snapped on his Maglight and ventured out into it. They walked straight through the heart of the field at the middle of the grounds. A thousand yards. Maybe more. They headed toward the museum, veered off to the right of it, and followed a well-crafted pathway that lead down to a cluster of huts. John smelled the river. He felt his ears stretch and strain for tiny sounds, real or imagined. In his mind, he was a native. Smudge-faced and musky, his body a sleek extension of the elements. He could not say why, but there was no doubt: he was glad he had joined Billy Ray.

Their rendezvous point was the middle hut in the near distance. Inside, a musty smell accompanied the pitch-black dark. Billy Ray lead the way, beaming light into every crevice. Right behind him, John shined his flashlight at the ground in front of him and wound his way through the partitions at the entrance.

Billy Ray's light revealed a birthing scene. The swarthy dummies looked the part, but only if you did not look too close. The stock-still midwife peered down at the young brown girl who held a bundle at her breast. The new mother lay flat on her back on a too-thin bench, a ratty cover draped over her. She looked sick, deathly, and maybe she was. But none of this seemed to concern her. Her eternal focus was the swaddled babe-in-arms. The warrior-father kneeled, proud and awed, at her side. The newborn's brother stood in the wings, gazing at his father, soaking up some vital instruction as to how he should comport himself in a far-off future that would never come.

"Over here, Governor," said a voice. It came from down low in the back corner of the hut. Billy Ray swung his beam of light over to it. A hairy little creature crouched near the ground on its haunches.

"Enough with the cloak and dagger shit," said Billy Ray. "You scared the hell out of me. I thought you were a cop. Or one of them dummies come to life."

Billy Ray put the Maglight on the ground with the beam shining upward. It cast just enough light for the three of them to see each other. Chewie took out a plastic bag and a box of papers and started rolling a joint.

"Wicked Buddy Hollys."

"He means your eyeglasses," said Billy Ray. He sat down cross-legged with a groan. "He likes them. That is what you mean, ain't it?"

"Roger that," said Chewie. "That's an affirmative in the *beaucoup*, over. Here, let me try." Chewie abandoned the joint he was rolling and reached up for John's glasses. John obliged and sat in the dim circle of light. He got close enough to smell Chewie. Black licorice. Sweet spices. Armpits.

"Holy shit, you are one blind fucking lieutenant. I have a profound new respect for you. You have persevered over great obstacles in life. This bodes well for your future. Stake out the untrodden path. A journey of a thousand miles begins with a single step. Eat more Chinese food. Only you can prevent forest fires."

Chewie handed the glasses over and went back to rolling.

"Don't worry," Billy Ray said to John. "He don't make a damn bit of sense until he tokes up. He's wound too tight otherwise."

"*Au contraire*," said Chewie. He feigned dismay, but he kept up with his industrious rolling. "I'm way looser than anybody you know. The grass just makes me timeless."

Billy Ray snorted at that and pulled a beer from the back of his pants. "Y'all two pussies don't want none of this I know, but I won't hold it against you. To each his own."

"Yes, sir, Dr. Cirrhosis," said Chewie. He had finished with the meticulous joint-craft. He pulled a lighter from his shirt pocket and held the joint out to Billy Ray.

"Let our guest go first," said Billy Ray.

This was a time-honored male tradition. Even John knew it. The new man must be tested. Is he sporting. Is he to be trusted. Is he willing to sublimate himself to the greater good: i.e., a collective good time. John had felt this sort of pressure before, but not the camaraderie that went with it. What else could he say but *yes*.

III

John found himself chest deep in the river. In all his clothes. The current was an insistent thing. He stumbled and he could not feel his head. It had unmoored itself, floated up to join the other astral bodies. And yet here he was, the rest of him, in a muddy river that was colder and swifter than he had expected it to be.

The moon was unabashedly bright and large. Its pockmarks on full display. He believed he could touch its powdery white surface, and he would have had it not meant reaching up, which would have meant losing his balance and being swept away forever.

"Don't float off," said Chewie. "We're over here."

Chewie had taken a different tack altogether. At the bank, he had stripped naked. Now he cut the current like a schooner, the tips of his long hair and beard submerged in the water as he dog-paddled around.

John trudged upstream through the many tons of moving water, slipping on the silty bottom. He searched out Billy Ray and spied him on the bank, squatted down, boots off, no shirt, jeans rolled at the ankles.

"Boys," said Billy Ray. "I've got something to say."

"Lieutenant, will you please quit your incessant yappety-yap? Fuckleberry Hinn has the floor," said Chewie.

"I apologize. I really do," said John, and Chewie laughed at him.

"It is official: I am now convinced you are the sweetest young man alive," said Chewie.

"Shut up, now. Both of you. I'm serious on this. This is serious."

John stopped where he was and leaned into the current.

Billy Ray picked at the mud and collected it into a small pie, which he tossed into the river. Then he regained his momentum.

"We're all called to something, are we not?"

"Abort, Chief," said Chewie. "This is headed down the dark corridor."

Billy Ray kept on.

"I have to believe we are," he said. "Chewie there's a spitting image of Yoko Ono, and that's got to count for something. John's probably got some kind of skill, even if he hadn't figured it out yet. Ginny's good at all kinds of things."

"What's your superpower?" asked Chewie.

"I win hearts and minds," said Billy Ray.

"Oh, that. I forgot."

"But here we all are at the fucking river," said Billy Ray. "Again. Stoned and drunk. Again."

"I'm not drunk," Chewie said.

"Neither am I," said John. "And Virginia's in the car."

"Fine. Stoned *and/or* drunk in the general vicinity of the river. That can't be a calling. That can't be the way we're supposed to spend the rest of our days. That's just playing out the fucking string."

Chewie swam and spurted river water while John did his best to stay upright. Billy Ray changed his line of questioning.

"How come this river always smells like shit?"

"That's not shit you smell," said Chewie. "That's life as

we know it. Fish guts and industrial waste and the sick water table."

Billy Ray dug at the mud and stewed some more. "Tell John-Boy what you are," he said.

Chewie backstroked downstream. "I am a ne'er do well, a prodigal son, a hairy nincompoop who endeavors to contribute to the dissolution of the last vestiges of order and decency in the world."

"No," said Billy Ray. "What you really are."

"Ah, you must be referring to my former life in the fast paced and stimulating field of the high maths." Chewie swam backwards against the current, so he was very nearly swimming in place. "But that's not what I really am. You believe me, don't you, Lieutenant? That can't possibly be all I really am."

"Yes, I do," said John. "I do believe you."

"No offense," said Billy Ray, "but you're a gullible fuck. Chewie there has been to more school than you and me and Ginny combined. He can make numbers tell you anything you want to know, and even some things you don't want to know."

"Garcon," said Chewie. "Check please."

"But here he is skinny dipping in a shit-stinkin' river in the middle of fucking nowhere," said Billy Ray. "And I want to know how it happened. Because if I know how it happened to him, I might know how it happened to me. And then I might be able to figure out what I should do with this bullshit mess my life is in."

Chewie circled around John and headed to the bank. He pulled his scrawny, naked frame up onto the shore and grabbed his pile of clothes. He did not stop to put them on. He just started the long climb back up the hill to the park.

"Any time I try to talk serious you just get all butt-hurt about it and go home. Is that it?"

"Affirmative," said Chewie. "*Should* is not a conversation that interests me. This my poor parents can confirm."

"You going naked?" said Billy Ray.

"I'll drip dry," said Chewie.

"Good idea," said Billy Ray. "That should get you into some interesting conversations."

"Wait," said John. "You can't go yet. I have to show you something."

With the exertion, John's equilibrium shifted. He made a move to the bank but the current was too much for him.

Chewie stopped climbing the hill. Billy Ray dropped his mud pie. "Show him something? What the hell you got to show *him*?"

"Now this," said Chewie, "is an intrigue."

John labored in the direction of the bank but his footing was hopeless. He felt himself give way and float with the current. The bank and his two companions on it were far away and getting farther. He might have shouted out for help but it did not occur to him. Instead he leaned back with his head toward the sky. All he could see was a black field scattered with stars. He gave in. The water rushed all around him and underneath him. There were voices from the bank but there was now a great chasm between where they were and where he was. The dark world floated by. He did not know he needed to be saved. Still, something saved him. It caught him by the leg. A slippery, pale fish. The faint smell of licorice and armpits. *Shit, Lieutenant*, said his unexpected savior, *I thought I told you not to float away?*

IV

The three of them slogged up the hill and through the interior of the park. John's clothes squished as he walked. Chewie had been persuaded to put on his pants even though his legs were still wet. Billy Ray had unrolled the bottoms of his jeans and he put his boots back on, but his good shirt was untucked and unbuttoned to his ribs. They seemed the worse for wear, a ragtag fragment of some shattered platoon, but John felt good, even with the trace remnants of river water in his lungs.

"I meant what I said back there," he said.

"What did you say back there?" asked Chewie. "It was all glug-glug sounds to me."

"I told you I got something to show you before you go."

"Noun or verb?" said Chewie.

"Noun," said John. "I don't have it here with me. It's in the car."

"If you mean Ginny, he don't like Ginny. And she don't like him."

"It's not her," said John.

They continued through the entrance to the park and traipsed back down the shoulder of the State Road. By the time they reached the Dairy Freeze lot, their hair was almost dry. They turned the corner of the building and Chewie stopped short. Ginny sat cross-legged on the hood of the Pinto.

"It's about damn time," she said. "I'm not even drunk anymore."

"I told you you were drunk," said Billy Ray. "Don't be scared of her, Chewie. She don't bite."

"Whose ride is this?" Chewie asked, almost under his breath.

"John's," said Virginia. "By way of his uncle."

"Your uncle?"

"You could say it that way," said John. "Yes."

"Let's see what you got to show," said Billy Ray. "You got me curious now."

"Who's got something to show?" said Virginia.

"John does," said Billy Ray. "Chewie fished him out of the river and now John's repaying his debt of gratitude."

"No wonder y'all smell like you do," said Virginia. "Anybody gets in that water on purpose ain't got the sense God gave them."

John fumbled in his pockets for the keys. For a split second he worried they might have floated away in the river, but there they were, buried in wet denim. After some time and effort, he got them out and put the proper key in the lock. Up sprang the hatch like some sarcophagus lid. All four of them gathered round.

It was dark and hard to see but they could smell it. Chewie backed away from the car and sat down on the curb. He dug his fists into both eyes, as if that could erase the dark forms he had just seen. The other three waited for him to spit out a verdict.

"I have to apologize," said Chewie, "I should've let the river take you."

Born Again

"Many survival case histories show that stubborn, strong
willpower can conquer many obstacles. One case history
tells of a man stranded in the desert for eight days
without food and water; he had no survival training,
and he did nothing right. But he wanted to survive, and
through sheer willpower, he did survive. With training,
equipment, and the will to survive, you will find you can
overcome any obstacle you may face. You will survive."
—*The U.S. Army Survival Manual*

*I was encased in a dark, safe womb. Warm fluid all around me and in me. And
then a terrible sucking sound and waves of strong pushing toward a trapdoor I had
not known was there.*

Out into the desert.

No survival training.

*And then there, at the point of entry into the world, was my father's face, a
jumbled, sinewy maw where the mouth used to be:* Good god, boy, I always
said you can't do nothing right and damned if I wasn't telling it
just exactly like it was. You won't last a second out here on your
own. Mark my goddamn words. Not a second.

Then me all alone in a slick heap on the parched ground. Spitting out lungfuls of brine.

The Intercessor

I

Chewie would have nothing to do with the final dispensation of Karl's automobile or his somewhat more than recreational stash of contraband. *Should* was not a conversation that interested him, but sometimes it could not be avoided. For the sake of self-preservation.

He had recognized the car as Karl's when he first saw it. The Pinto was bright, loud, one of a kind. No question it was Karl's. Someone peddling any kind of contraband in Karl's sphere of influence knew to avoid him. Karl was mean and violent even when he hadn't been wronged. In this case, his pursuit would be relentless, and he would arrive at the point of contact in no mood to go easy.

"I don't know why you did it or how you did it, but I do know Karl Adams and that means I know the word for the situation you're in," Chewie said. "*Untenable.*"

Chewie got up from the curb and put his arm around John.

"*Fucked*," said Chewie. "That is more or less the vernacular equivalent." Chewie flipped his soggy shirt over his shoulder and started to walk away.

"I know what it means," said John.

"Excellent," said Chewie. "Knowing the problem is half the battle."

"Don't you even want a ride to your car?" asked Billy Ray.

Chewie kept walking. "Negative with extreme unction on the offer of transport," said Chewie. He broke into a half jog. "Best to splinter, disappear into the countryside without a trace. Let the storm pass. This is a hereditary skill. Over and out. Don't call me, I'll call you. Et cetera."

He turned the corner around the Dairy Freeze and was gone. Billy Ray reached down into the trunk and pulled up a bag stuffed full of marijuana. He held it close to his face, trying to get as much light on it as he could, but there was only one streetlamp and it was a hundred feet away. He sniffed the bag and then tossed it back in the trunk.

"Looks like we got ourselves a predicament," he said.

II

They could not ride with the windows rolled up because the river funk was too bad. It steamed the windows. The night air was cool and it served to blow some of the stink off of John and Billy Ray. John drove but his head did not feel right, and so he went slow and tried to stay on the right side of the double yellow line. He was mostly successful. In the front seat, Billy Ray stared out the window and rubbed his chin in the pose of a thinker. Virginia sat quiet in the back, but John felt her eyes on him. They got back to the trailer and the whole park was still. That far out in the country, there was no ambient light. John could not see his feet and he stumbled up the stairs to the deck.

"Easy now," said Billy Ray. "Ain't no use breaking your neck. Especially with a mean old drug dealer ready and willing to do it for you."

The three of them walked single file into the trailer. The television was on and Momma was in her recliner but she was sleeping. Her head lolled to one side and her thin-lipped mouth hung open. Billy Ray took the remote from her lap and switched off the TV.

"Time to hit the hay, old girl," said Billy Ray. He jostled her shoulder some and she came to. She seemed frightened at first and then angry to be awakened. Momma yawned and displayed the foul inner workings of her mouth. She strained to get up from the seat and shuffled past Billy Ray, only pausing to scowl when she smelled him. After a trip to the hall bathroom, where she peed without closing the door or turning on the light or flushing it away, she went to her room. Without a word and with authority, she shut the door on them.

John sat at the card table that served as a place for meals. Billy Ray pulled a blanket and a pillow from the hall closet.

"I tell you what," said Billy Ray. "I was wrong when I said you were a gullible fuck. Or maybe you are one, but you're a mystery man, too. That's something else altogether." He gave John a soft punch on the shoulder, tossed the bedding on the couch, and started back down the hall.

"You coming to bed?" he said to Virginia.

"In a minute," she said. "Go on and get your shower and I'll be in there when you get out."

"Don't stay up too late, you kids," said Billy Ray as he kept walking. "Christ if I'm not getting too old for such excitement." He gave a half-hearted wave and shut the bedroom door behind him.

Ginny chose her words with unusual care.

"You may think I do like we did earlier with just anybody, anytime, but I don't," she said. "I like you because you say things the way they are, plain and simple. But maybe it's what you don't say that I have to worry about. And there's a lot you don't say."

"If I told you everything," said John, "you wouldn't believe it."

"Try me," she said.

Virginia's eyes were red from alcohol and fatigue. But they were honest and ready to receive him, so he told her. His father, with and without a face. The way it felt to pull the trigger. They way it felt to know he could not take it back, and how he didn't want to anyway, even if he could. He told her about

Duckworthy, Karl, Professor H. All the sad men. As true and as clear and as far back as his memory would let him. He told her everything and she did not flinch. When they got up to go to bed, she took him in her arms.

"It's fine now," she told him, "because you're with us."

She walked away from him, down the hall. The light in the bedroom was off. The door was closed. She touched her hand to the knob and then turned back around to face him. Her face a faint but unmistakable invitation.

The Trinity

The points of contact three bodies share on a warm, wet night. Six limbs, seven openings, one empty womb. Any number of possible ends. No words because words would make it something other than an Otherworld, a dream. This hand reaches in the dark. Two mouths search out a slim finger. The rough rub of an eyebrow across a full bottom lip. The earth's surface is a precarious field of moving bodies. Sliding, shifting. They collide, turn in or up, and come apart. Species and souls congregate on the wide new continent—a string of millennia feels infinite, like a promise—and then one day they find themselves marooned on separate shards of land. Undulating saltwater in all directions. They begin again.

This is the place of origin.

Mountains form at the place where two or more bodies meet. Somewhere in a dream a series of knees forms a promontory for an epochal instant. Time enough for the insignificant sentients in the shadows, the hollows, the valleys and caves to devise prayers, demons, an intricate literature of lies to explain who made the mountain and why.

This is mythmaking.

Three bodies in the bed in the silence. Curling into one another, leaning back away. Three bodies making shapes. Making letters, an alphabet, a language. Three bodies dizzy in the heat and the wet.

One concept of time holds that this leads to that, one after another, in a recognizable sequence. One person—a soul, a mind, a heart—cannot be in two places at once. And so on.

Three bodies meet at a single point in time: one warm, wet night.

Another concept of time holds that a universe of happenings lives and dies in the very same instant. Now holds an entire history. Now is a prophecy, a promise. What never happened, what no one remembers, what someone else dreamed. When and where and why and how are always immaterial. Anything infinite is unfathomable. Anything infinite turns back in upon itself.

Sacred Ground

John woke with Billy Ray's mother hovering over him like a blank-faced but curious child. When she realized he was awake, she spirited away from him as if he could not see her, as if she believed she was invisible. She padded down the hall. In the kitchen there were scraping and stirring noises, the occasional sound of the faucet running or dishes clanging in the sink. He pulled on his pants and went to it.

"How you want your eggs this morning, Momma? Now that's just a joke, to see if you're paying attention. Anybody don't know you like the yolk cooked hard all the way through, well, they just don't know my Momma."

The smell of eggs too long in the pan came over John in a wave and it almost made him sick. He himself was rank and all he wanted to do was get clean.

"Look who's up and at 'em," said Billy Ray. He was crisp and ready for the day, with a clean-shaven jaw line and his hair combed back just so. He pointed the spatula he was holding at the coffee maker.

"There's your joe, if you take it," he said.

"I'd like a shower," said John.

"Knock yourself out. There's towels in the closet. Use Momma's bathroom. It ain't her bath day, so she won't care."

Momma looked up from her plate of eggs when she heard her name. The glare she shot John suggested that maybe she did care after all. Billy Ray brought her some ketchup, though, and her attention was diverted long enough for John to sneak past her.

"You need a change of clothes?"

"I think I might have to burn those others," said John.

"I don't guess we're a perfect fit, but I might have something that'll come close. I'll have them for you when you get out, and some eggs. How you like them?"

"Scrambled," said John. "Thank you."

John headed for the shower and Billy Ray scraped the residue from Momma's eggs out of the pan and pulled out three more for scrambling.

"I been thinking about our little problem," Billy Ray called after him. "And I got some ideas. It's like old Coach Kight used to say back in high school. Every challenge is just an opportunity in disguise."

John was familiar with this line of reasoning from the quote book, though he had not yet seen it borne out in his own experience. Time would tell, he supposed. He made his way into the bathroom. Soon he stood naked in a sharp stream of hot water. He sudsed and scrubbed and shampooed. It felt better than he expected to be clean. As he toweled himself dry, he smelled the food again, but this time it made him hungry. He was ready to eat, he was ready get out in the sun and the heat of the day, he was ready for things to happen.

———

Already the television was on and Momma was stationed in her recliner when John emerged. The pants Billy Ray had placed outside the bathroom door were too long for him, so he rolled them up, but the threadbare t-shirt was nearly a proper fit. He had his toast and eggs and a glass of milk, then Billy Ray poured himself some more coffee and invited him out to his office, which meant the deck. It was already warm and sticky outside, but the trailer itself and the mimosa tree gave them some shade.

Billy Ray leaned back in his white plastic chair and propped himself against the house.

"How them clothes treat you?" he asked.

John nodded. "It feels good to be rid of that river."

Billy Ray nodded back, sipped his black coffee, and breathed deep. "Today is a good day. I can feel it. Ain't nothing bad can happen today."

John wanted to know what made him think that for sure. Because he had never believed such a thing about any day. Not even this one, which he, too, liked the feel of so far. Before he could ask Billy Ray more about it, there was a stirring in the woods just beyond the tracks.

"Morning, Mr. Mose," called Billy Ray. "You striking out into the day?"

Mose climbed up onto the tracks and shaded his eyes with his hand.

"Right Reverend out early today," said Mose.

"Yes, sir," said Billy Ray. "Got to when you're solving the problems of the world. Come on over here and meet my friend John."

Mose stayed where he was and gave John the same hi-sign he had given him the day before. "Good to know you," he said. "Best be getting on before it get too hot. You tell the Man?"

"I haven't seen him since I last saw you," said Billy Ray. "But I'm going to see him later today. He'll be glad to hear you're ready for him again. He gets anxious when he hasn't seen you for a while."

"It's hard work birthing things into the world," said Mose.

"I imagine so," said Billy Ray. "The Man'll be out to see you. I'll be sure to tell him."

Mose raised his hand again in acknowledgment and made his way down the tracks, his walking stick tamping at the gravel like it reminded him where the earth was.

"He called you Reverend," said John. "He did it yesterday too."

"Old Mose is an odd bird," said Billy Ray. "Says he sees things before they happen, and he says he seen me one time preaching to the multitudes. So now he calls me Reverend. No harm in it. Have to say I even like it."

"What man is he talking about?"

"Mose paints pictures," said Billy Ray. "Folks with money they don't know what to do with, they think he's a backwoods genius. I say it's a long shot, but lots of folks do crazier shit than buy up an old black man's pictures and put them on their walls. There's a man in town helps him sell it. He's a man that knows a lot of people, a lot of things. I thought we might go see him about what you got in your trunk, so you can meet him later on. If you're interested in seeing what he has to say about it, that is. Means going back where you came from. He owns a bar in town. The Bastille."

"Karl haunts that place," said John.

"Maybe just me and Ginny should go then."

"It's my problem. I'll go. You trust this man?" said John.

"As much as I trust anybody," said Billy Ray. "Which ain't a whole lot. I think he'll tell us straight."

Billy Ray downed the dregs of his coffee. The door cracked open and Virginia came out. Her hair was mussed and her eyes were bleary and she came over to sit on Billy Ray's lap.

"Why's everybody out here?" she said, rubbing her eyes.

"You are an angel of the morning, you are," said Billy Ray, and he nuzzled her neck. "You want some eggs?"

"Uh-huh," she said and she yawned.

"Well we ain't got none because Johnny over there ate 'em all."

"Good," she said. "You need it, bony as you are. I'll go fix a bowl of cereal." She took the empty mug from Billy Ray's hands and got up. On her way past, she mussed John's clean hair then disappeared back into the trailer.

"You must have done something right," said Billy Ray. "Eat up all her eggs and she don't even care. Must be those lost-puppy eyes you got. I'd let you eat my eggs too."

John liked the teasing. Virginia soon came out with her bowl of flakes and more coffee for Billy Ray. She again took her perch on her man's lap. The three of them sat in silence while Virginia ate and the temperature climbed. The day was in front of them, and though he did not know what it would come of it, John believed for once he was right where he belonged.

———

There was the matter of securing the contraband. Carting it around made Billy Ray nervous. It was his idea to bury it. They waited for the sun to go down that night, then he and John drove back out to the Mounds. Virginia did not like the idea, it being state property.

"That's just it," said Billy Ray. "Won't nobody think to look for it there. Plus it's protected by Benevolent Spirits. That place has always been good to me."

Virginia rolled her eyes and washed her hands of it. The two of them spirited into the park again and took off their shirts to dig a great hole. Billy Ray wielded a pick axe and John scooped out shovels full of red dirt in the woods just off the river. It was just a kitchen garbage bag half full of dope, but they buried it like a living body. With care and solemnity.

Later, in the shower, before they all three went out for the night, the dirt from the dig rinsed off John's body in a deep, red residue. Red from the iron in the ground. Like blood is red from the very same source.

II

Visionary

This is a black man out in the woods. The great, quiet woods. Once he knew two women at once. The wiry hair on their heads and between their legs. He liked to rest his head on their wide soft stomachs. When he was a young man he ached for women and the smell of them was everywhere. His fingers and his own thighs. The smell of them was in the trees. In the wet ground. These two he knew were wonderful black women. Bigger than him and rounder than him and their smell stuck to him and to everywhere they ever were.

This is a black man out in the woods. This is a black man out in the woods alone.

He mixes his paints.

This is a black man out in the woods alone mixing his paints. He loves the dizzy smell. Yellow ochre. Burnt sienna. Phthalo blue. Titanium white. These colors that never change. Profound and unnatural. Nothing like a tree. Nothing like how a tree is a hundred different colors and all its unnamed shades. Nothing like how a tree becomes newly colored in each new day, every hour. Even a minute is a new saturation. Nothing like the way a beautiful black woman is a shifting palette of everything but black. Behind her knees a color. Her palms a color, a color the same color as the soles of her feet. The skin stretched over her kneecap a color. Her nose and ears a color. Her lips. And the deep red pink inside of her.

Now he paints undulations. Rhythms and echoes. In every shade of brown that can be made or be dreamed.

This is a black man out in the woods.

He mixes his paints. He paints all morning on a stack of flat slate sheets. The Man brings the sheets. He paints until the smell and his hunger become too much. His small cabin. A low ceiling. He goes to the kitchen, warms the stove. The smack and smell of fried lunch meat. A cracked egg in the same pan. The yellow and the pink and the steam that is rich with pig fat and the metal smell of a yolk. He scrapes it onto a plate and eats the whole mess of it with salt and water. He has washed the pan and his one plate, his one fork, taken up his one palette again before he remembers that he cannot remember the last words he said out loud or when he said them or to whom.

The second woman was a dream. Like the afterlife. The blossom of bush on her head. Her soft form. She was younger than him, almost still a child. She engulfed him. He let himself be engulfed by her. He could smell her on him for days.

The second woman was the second coming. Now even she—especially she—is gone.

When the smell of the paints is too much, he finds a clearing in the woods, where the vast sky opens up. He gathers heavy stones. Puts them in a certain order. According to their shape, their size. If they are flat, if they are smooth. If they are rounded, oblong, like a heart muscle. He moves them like game pieces, and when he stands away they are slow moving creatures. They are dancing a dance this world moves too fast to see.

The first woman had places on her so light they looked like they were made of the moon.

This is a black man out in the woods. Alone. The night is cool and the sky is black and there is a cloud of stars. He leans his new paintings up against the far wall. Prisoners before a firing squad. Suspects to be identified by the aggrieved. Maybe they are noble, tired women in a brothel. Migrants looking for work. When they go they are gone and they never look back. Their smell stuck to him and to everywhere they ever were. Everything he has ever made or known an orphan.

The Underworld

The bar was not a happy place. It was tucked away in a sleepy section of the college town, near the courthouse and the municipal jail. A place you had to know to look for. It was early evening and the orange streetlamps fought the dusk. A day's worth of heat still rose from the ground. Billy Ray crossed the empty street hand-in-hand with Virginia, John a few steps behind. He was lost in the gaudy mural on the bar's façade and he paused in front of it as the other two went inside. Images of the Sistine Chapel. Adam reaching for a white-haired God. Moses and his tablets. Noah's drunkenness. Also the French Revolution, the words LIBERTE, FRATERNITE, EGALITE in bold baroque letters above the door.

Inside, it was an island of misfit toys: one man dragged himself across the cement floor wearing catcher's leggings to protect the stubs he had for legs. A walleyed man threw darts—with precision—by himself. Many of the people were tattooed and pierced. An atmosphere of ritual scarification.

In addition to the dartboards there was a pool table, dormant. And the stink of stale beer and mildew. There was also original art for sale hanging on the walls. Self-taught in style. Apocalyptic in theme. A great many flames and birds and dark night skies. Up on the small stage a young man played a guitar and sang in a rough warble. His playing was not good or bad, and almost no one in the bar was listening. When he finished a song, one woman clapped but he did not acknowledge her. He leaned down, picked up a bottle of beer at his feet, and took two swallows. Then he moved into another song, oblivious to the all-encompassing oblivion around him.

This was the one bar where Billy Ray chose to be known. When he presented himself, they welcomed him with a few dead grunts and imperceptible nods. Most times he had Virginia on his arm. They liked that Virginia was on an arm in the place.

"It's the fundamental principles of this establishment," he had explained to John on the way over. "Any common man can conquer anything that stands in his way."

And yet everyone in the place appeared to be conquered.

"That your new friend?" said the man behind the bar. John had hung back, just inside the door, to admire a painting of a fish. The bartender was shave-headed, an inky tattoo on his face and one circumnavigating his neck.

"That is indeed," said Billy Ray. "He ready for him?"

"He is," said the bartender.

John joined them. "I like those pictures," he said.

"You want to buy one?" asked the bartender. "Here lately we can't give the sumbitches away. I tell him, folks don't like to be reminded of all the evil they got coming, but the Man thinks it's genius. Says if anybody knows what Hell looks like, it'd be an old black man who lives out in the woods. Truth is both of 'em's apeshit crazy."

The man on stage wailed and his guitar belched feedback.

"Wolfie's in rare form this evening," said Billy Ray.

"Got in his cups early tonight," said the bartender. "Apartment fire where he lives. Lost everything, LPs and all. Neighbor downstairs got burned up in it."

"That's awful," said Virginia. "Why is he even here? I'd go crawl up in a ball someplace if that happened to me."

"When things go to shit, there's something to be said for your daddy owning a place like this and all the spirits in it."

The bartender put a full pitcher of beer on the bar along with three clear plastic cups. Virginia threaded her arm through the crook in Billy Ray's elbow.

"I think I might have a white wine."

"You some kind of movie star now?" said Billy Ray.

"I got a taste for something different is all. I'm allowed to want what I want."

"I know what you got a taste for," he said. "Showing off your Audrey Hepburn. Ain't it enough for you to smell so damn sweet and have your lips all shiny and swish your little behind the way you do in that get-up?"

Virginia set her pretty jaw. "Never mind then," she said. "I need to go powder my nose. If you'll excuse me."

"Powder your nose? Put on your airs all you want to. It's out of the frying pan, into the fire, you ask me."

She stomped off. The bartender shared a smile with Billy Ray.

"Got to keep them on their toes," Billy Ray said. He nudged John.

"I'll take your word for it," said John.

Billy Ray grabbed the pitcher and the cups and headed toward the back of the bar.

"Tell Wolfie where we're at when he gets down off of there."

II

Venturing into the bowels of the place, near the bathrooms, they came to a staircase. Further down the dark hallway, a door opened out into a courtyard in the back. Billy Ray thrust his chin up toward the top of the stairs.

"Go on," he said. "He's waiting. We'll be out back when he's through with you."

"I thought you were coming too," said John.

"He don't want to see me," said Billy Ray. "Never more than one person up there at a time. Divide and conquer is how he rolls."

The staircase was narrow and dark, darker as he climbed. Halfway up, he could not see in front of him. There was no railing, so John ran his hand along the rough wall to keep his bearings. When he got to the landing, his eyes had adjusted. The space was tight. To his left was a fuse box and straight ahead was a door. A thin band of light leaked through the crack at the bottom. He brought his fist up to the door but hesitated with his knuckles inches away. On the other side of those three inches of laminate particle board was a bubble cordoned off from everything around it. Sequestered but somehow, still, lording over it. He had not ever been in such a place. A perch removed from the smoke and noise and heat of life, where someone could sit and think and, in a pocket of calm, decide the course of everything down below. He had not believed, prior to this, that such places existed. One knock and he would forfeit yet another small piece of his sustaining ignorance.

"You just going to stand out there and mouth-breathe? Come on in or leave me alone."

The door was less heavy than he expected it to be. It almost swung out of his hand when he opened it. The room was like a cave, with a ceiling much higher than what he would have thought and a damp chill to the place. Exposed duct work hummed above them. There were three different sources of light. A small green-shaded banker's lamp cast a full radius of light on a cluttered desktop. On the far wall, a wide window let in the rose tinge from the bar below. On the wall closest to the door were four inset security monitors, all of them on, all of them emitting a gray-white pall. A man with his longish white hair pulled back in a ponytail sat in a swivel chair with his back to the door. He wore black Chuck Taylor tennis shoes, which were propped on the window ledge, and he stared out into the smoky red glow. He did not turn to greet his visitor, even after John closed the door behind him.

"Already I know some things about you," said the Man. "Haven't quite pieced it all together yet, but I figure you got a problem and I suspect it's bigger than you are."

He took a pack of cigarettes from the pocket of his black t-shirt. He removed one with exaggerated care and lit it with a match. He extinguished the flame with one hard shake and turned to John with a raised his eyebrow. He wore a white goatee and his face was ruddy and pocked.

"What do you know about me?" the Man asked.

"You might help me figure things out," said John. "And I gather you like to buy paintings. That's all."

"How old are you?" said the Man.

"Nineteen," said John.

"No good reason for anybody that age to know anything at all." The Man stood up and revealed himself to be barrel-chested, tall and strong and more vital than his years would seem to allow. He scanned the office and walked out from behind the desk, searching everywhere with patient intensity. A long nose and a prominent brow gave him the look of a large predatory bird. On a small table near John, he found what he was looking for. An ashtray. He covered the distance in three broad, heavy steps. He ashed into the palm-sized glass container then carried it back over to his desk.

"I want to show you something," he said. "Look down there."

It was just the barroom, but from this angle it was transformed into a hive of slow-moving creatures bathed in red light. Arms shuttled cups of one thing or another to an assortment of mouths and back again to where they had rested before. Someone got up, broke off from the mass, headed to take a piss. Another went the other way, out past the pool table, toward the door and an aimless night spent somewhere else. On the small black stage, the young man played. His eyes shut tight, the chords at his neck stretched tight and earnest. None of this made a sound that they could hear. John had just come from there, but here, above it, sealed off, it seemed like a foreign country or worse. It seemed like a warren of some burrowing horde of blind animals.

"My son," he said, "sounds like shit. I let him play here because no place else will have him."

"I'm sure he appreciates it," said John.

"He hates me for it," said the Man. "Any self-respecting man that age hates the man that raised him. Probably that's vice versa.

It goes double when the younger man has no discernable talents." He sat again and the chair groaned under him. John kept his eyes fixed on the scene below because he did not want to have to meet the Man's gaze. All of a sudden, he wished he hadn't come. It seemed sure that nothing good could come of this.

"You've got a sales and distribution problem," the Man said. Cigarette smoke leaked from his nostrils.

John swallowed hard and found a chair on the other side of the desk. He sat on the edge of the seat like a schoolboy. "I guess I should tell you the whole story."

"I'd rather you not," said the Man.

"What do you want to know then?"

"There's three things in general I already know," said the Man. He held up his hand and raised a finger to enumerate each one. "One: most everybody is for shit. Two: nothing in this world hasn't happened before. Three: it's best to keep to what you know."

The Man leaned back in his chair and put his feet up on the desk. His cigarette lay smoldering in the ashtray, a thin trail of smoke snaking its way up until it dissipated into a general gray cloud above their heads.

"Start with the first principle," said the Man. He picked up the butt and took a deep final drag, then he stubbed it out. "Your friends like you and that counts for something. But it doesn't count for much. I feel obliged to tell you that your association with these particular people will lead to no good end. Not when it comes to this."

The Man opened a drawer and pulled out a remote control. He pointed it at one of the screens on the opposite wall, the grainy image flickering from a view of the empty back alley to that of the courtyard. Slumped on a bench was a shirtless figure John did not recognize. Billy Ray sat opposite him, sipping from a cup of beer and staring at the door. Waiting, stale and rudderless, for something—anything—to happen.

"How do you know it's not the other way around?" said John. "It could be me that's the bad influence."

"Exactly right. You're for shit too," said the Man. "But that doesn't mean you picked the right folks to have in your corner with this mess you got yourself into. You won't be able to get out of each other's way."

"I thought that was where you came in," said John. "They brought me to you for help."

The Man chuckled and went to his shirt pocket for another cigarette. "I peddle booze and art because I like booze and art. I don't mess with anything else because whenever I have, it sooner or later goes to hell. Mostly sooner."

John looked back to the screen. Billy Ray was right where he had been, as if he was in stop-frame but the shirtless figure swayed every now and then so it was clear the image was still moving in real time.

"My boy's apartment building got burned up today," said the Man. "You want to know why?"

John kept his eyes on the flickering gray image of Billy Ray. He had an inkling, but he didn't have the nerve to say it.

"I know the man you're at odds with, maybe even better than you do. You know as well as I do he comes in here more nights than not. Right about this time. That makes this one of the worst places you could be, and it means you're either reckless or stupid to come here. Or it means you're nineteen, which means you're reckless *and* stupid. This man is ignorant and he's mean, and that's the kind of man who's got nothing to lose in scorching the earth when he feels he's been wronged. It's just a shitty car and little bit of dope, but now he's got no reason to stop at you. He'll go one by one and take his pound of flesh from everyone and everything that's affronted him. Right out in the open. So you know what's coming."

John's mind churned.

"It was a teacher at the college that got burned up. Had a little black dog. Maybe you already figured that out by now."

The Man got up and walked over to the screen. Two new figures appeared. His son and Virginia had joined Billy Ray at the table. There they sat, smoking cigarettes and looking small. The Man tapped the screen.

"Best thing you can do for them," he said, "and for you, is to get as far away from here as you can, just as fast as you can get there. You stay, it won't end pretty. Probably won't end pretty anyway. But at least that way your conscience is clear."

John removed his glasses and rubbed his eyes. His insides were on fire. He felt his face flush and he had an urge to smash everything he saw.

"That's quite a war face you got worked up," said the Man. "But it's not near enough. I don't care what you've done in this life, you're not criminal enough to make this right on your own."

"You're saying that you won't help me," said John.

"I'm telling you how to help yourself and anybody you care even a little bit about," said the Man. "I'm telling you to run like hell and don't look back."

III

John made his way down the narrow staircase and into the nook that lead to the bathrooms. Undifferentiated sound blared from the bar: music and people, the occasional thump of a dart burying into cork. He entered the men's room and the sound abated. Bold graffiti—some of it artful, much of it scatological—covered every inch of the limited wall space. There was a toilet and a urinal and a sink, all jammed so close together, only two of them could be used at one time. John knelt before the toilet and wrapped his arms around the bowl. He was dizzy and his mouth felt sticky. A slow dry heave rumbled through him, nothing more. The door opened. Sound surged in then died away again as the door slammed shut. John stayed where he was, breathing in the residual smell of urine. In his peripheral vision, he could see a smooth bare leg. He followed it down to the floor and saw that it was attached to a foot in a red, open-toed high heel. A woman in tight cut-off jeans and a red camisole. Shapely, smooth. Her skin shiny and golden. She worked at her belt in front of the urinal, dug into her shorts, and produced an uncircumcised penis, longish and thick. She let out her bold stream and, with it, a deep groan. John averted his eyes. When she was through she went to the sink and teased her hair in the mirror. She leaned in, applied some lipstick, puckered her lips and pressed them together.

"I feel for you," she said. "Long night if that's where you're starting out." Her voice was soft and warm. "You want me to send somebody in to look after you?"

John shook his head.

"Suit yourself," she said. "I'd stay and help but I'm fixing to get laid and it's been a *long* time. You sure you're going to be okay?"

He nodded and as she left, the momentary sound from the bar belched in again. John knelt for a while longer in the relative silence before he got to his feet. He stood at the mirror, removed his glasses, rinsed his face, and then pressed out into the loud, hot smoke that waited on the other side of the door.

Lamentation

What I see is a terrible
Angel astride a swift,
strong steed. The rider
is winged. He rises, soars.
The beast rides on.
Who was it who sent this
after me—There must
be some Higher Power.
This can only end ugly.
One of us will be hanged.
The other ripped apart.
God Almighty an accessory,
slinking from the scene.

Lone Rider on a Pale Horse

I

Karl's philosophy of dispute resolution made an accounting of both compensatory and punitive damages. Thus the all-encompassing fire. Thus, likewise, on a smaller scale, the utter lack of embarrassment—much less remorse—in having commandeered a pimply adolescent's dun-colored motor scooter, on which he had no doubt spent hours combing the landscape, hunting down what was rightfully his: retribution and recompense by any and all necessary means.

A puny gray motor scooter has the dual advantage of being tied down and going unnoticed. And so there it was, chained to a telephone pole outside the counterculture bar, still warm from its all-day ride. John stormed past it, unawares, though he now knew for certain that he was fast approaching the confluence of his former and present lives.

Two sparsely populated blocks down from the bar, the Pinto was parallel parked between a rusted out van with two flat tires and a Pontiac Firebird with no windshield. The Scylla and Charybdis of inconsequence. John hurried to the Pinto and got in. He turned the ignition. It took two or three turns to rev the engine, but when it did, the Pinto grumbled its loud grumble. He lurched out of the tight spot and maneuvered the car down the street, coaxing it into its glacial manner of acceleration.

Virginia ran out of the bar and into the Pinto's path. She stopped in the middle of the street and threw her arms up in the air to stop him. He did not see an alternative, so he hit the brakes. The car stalled out with a shudder.

"You can't leave," she said. She slung the door open and got in. "I thought we were kindred spirits. I thought you were one of us now."

"Something came up," said John. He turned his attention to getting the car started again.

"I'll go with you," she said. "I'm good at taking care of things."

"What about Billy Ray?" asked John.

"He can take care of himself for a little while," she said. "Besides, this place bores me to kingdom come. I got a good buzz on and now I'm ready for something different. Show me the way."

"That man said it's not safe for anybody to be with me right now."

"If it's not safe for us then it's not safe for you. I don't see the sense in being unsafe all alone."

"You didn't ask for any of this," said John.

"Neither did you."

"Stealing cars is one sure way to attract trouble," said John.

"That doesn't even count," she said. "You had no other choice."

John did not have time to argue. He turned the key in the ignition and was greeted with another disheartening wheeze. The door to the bar opened and out came Billy Ray.

"You know what it is," said Virginia, pointing to the gauges. "It's out of gas. See. I'm helping already. Where would you be without me, that's what I'd like to know."

John slumped down and rested his head on the steering wheel. Billy Ray approached the car and leaned into Virginia's open window. He smiled a big drunk smile.

"Wherever we're headed to now," he said, "looks like we're walking."

II

The trio of drunkards—just plain drunk or drunk on fear and revelation—made its slow way down the tree-lined residential street. John shouldered his backpack, which was all he could salvage from the dead car. The three did not know what was behind them. Or they did but they could not know how close it was.

They trudged through a neighborhood that was a quilt of different sensibilities, different stations, different lives. A thick layer of leaves and branches formed a canopy overhead. Intermittent orange light from the streetlamps juxtaposed against deep black shadows. At regular intervals were large two-story houses with porches and well-kept yards. There were garden apartments, too, and occasional small duplex shacks, most in various states of disrepair, where students lived. Here and there, some stray animal, virtually wild, circled, poked out its head, went back to whatever it was doing in the first place. All of this bathed in pale orange light and shadow.

Of the three of them, Virginia weaved the most; she and Billy Ray had been drinking for hours. It was their custom to start just before the sun went down, and by the darker hours such as this, they had achieved the peak of their respective altered states. For Virginia, that meant weaving, but with a fluid kind of grace. Her boots slowed her down, so she kicked them off and carried them.

"You're gonna rip those pretty feet up," said Billy Ray. "We can't have that."

She ignored him and took an extra step every now and again to keep up with the insistent pace John was setting.

Billy Ray took the opportunity to fill the silence.

"You ever endeavor to sing?" he said. "I don't mean in the shower or something like that. In a chorus or something. A proper communal effort to make a joyful noise unto the world."

John quickened his pace. Billy Ray kept on.

"I bet you're all from the nasal cavity," he said. "That's how it is with most people who don't know better."

John kept walking, eyes forward. The three of them proceeded into an extended area of darkness, crowned by a row of thick, old oaks.

"Sometimes," said Virginia, "I think you don't have a clue about whatever the hell's happening in the world around you. It's just all you and nothing else. You're a Chatty Cathy, is what you are."

"Oh, my love, you get so mean to your old man when you get drunk. What did I ever do to you but cherish and love and honor and obey?"

Virginia snorted and shook her head. "That's what that's called?"

"Anyhow," said Billy Ray, "what I was saying before to Johnny here is that it's in the guts. That's the secret. You ever see them little Viennese fellows, you'll know just what I'm talking about. My lord they belt it out so large and sharp! It's because they find it in their guts and push it out. Everything's in the guts."

Billy Ray jogged ahead of them until he got to the next patch of light. There he turned to walk backwards and spread his arms wide, in the pose of a proclamation.

"And I'll tell you what, boys and girls," he said. "I've got me an announcement to make. I know just what it is I'm going to do from here on out."

"If it ain't a vow of silence, I don't want to hear it," said Virginia. John just kept moving on a bee-line toward something only he could know.

"I'm gonna get me a Preacher Show," said Billy Ray, undeterred, "just like Momma said I should, and I'm gonna get the biggest choir of little boys there ever was, and they are going to belt it out so to fill a great big arena named after me. It's gonna be a fucking hoot, I promise you. I'll even let you two be on TV if you want to."

Virginia stopped right where she was in the dark street.

"Can't you quit?" she said. "Nobody cares. We're *involved* in something here."

Billy Ray's face turned puzzled, and he stopped his backwards walk.

"Are we involved in something, Johnny?" he asked. "I thought we were just walking."

"I tell you what," said Virginia. She had staked her ground in the dark patch. "I got some big news to share, too. Nobody knows what the hell you're talking about half the time, and when they do, it just proves what they thought already, and that is you're half apeshit crazy. Just like your momma."

John kept up his march past Billy Ray, whose posture and expression had changed in an instant.

"I don't think I heard you right," he said.

"You heard me," said Virginia, still defiant but her voice was quieter and John could barely hear her as the distance between them grew. He heard Billy Ray storm after her, and he heard Virginia shriek and run in the opposite direction. Billy Ray's long stride overcame her easily. She threw her boots at him as he grabbed her. John kept marching.

Virginia kicked and punched and yelled for help. Billy Ray did his best to overpower her but his inebriated limbs were slow to carry out what his mind intended, and Virginia was strong and long herself. It was a struggle to subdue her.

"Hold still and hush up," he said, but Virginia did not listen. She clocked him in the mouth. A solid blow. Billy Ray absorbed the punch and tried to grab her arms. Her elbow struck him in the ear, and at that, he smacked her back without much pomp. She fell immediately in a heap, crying in one loud sob. Billy Ray scooped her up over his shoulder. She cried and screamed and pounded on his back with her fists.

"You hit me, you fucking redneck piece of shit!" she screamed.

"I had to defend myself," shouted Billy Ray. "Hold still or I'm going to end up dropping your ass on the pavement."

"Don't you ever fucking hit me!" She aimed her fists at what she thought might be his kidneys and she pounded, again and again, with all the strength she could conjure up.

Through all of this, John kept up his steady march.

III

He could smell it before he saw the smoldering shell. Yellow police tape ringed the perimeter. Two police officers stood outside to guard the place amidst the low, lullaby backdrop of walkie-talkie babble. John crouched behind a row of cars on the opposite side of the street, a safe distance away.

Billy Ray limped up a few moments later, winded, and laid Virginia on the grass next to the curb. She was nearly passed out from the exertion and all the stirred-up alcohol in her blood. When she was spread out on the ground, she moaned and, though it was dark where they were, she shaded her eyes in the crook of her elbow and then lay still as a corpse. Billy Ray stood tall and took in the destruction across the street.

"It'll be a miracle if I can keep from puking after all that. I'm too damn old for this shit."

He checked his lip. His mouth was bleeding from Virginia's roundhouse. He put his hands on his knees and spat a sticky mixture of saliva and mucous and blood onto the ground. A thin residual stream of it swayed from his bottom lip, and he wiped it away.

"Get down behind the car," said John. "And hush."

"It ain't against the law to collect myself."

John grabbed hold of Billy Ray's wrist.

"I didn't ask anybody to come with me," he said. "You can at least keep quiet while I do what I have to do."

Billy Ray grudgingly bent down onto his haunches. He stared down at the spot of ground between his boots.

"I do hate to vomit," he said.

"If you have to, do it quiet," said John. He adjusted his glasses and poked his head back over the hood of the car.

Billy Ray kept his head down and breathed steady for a while, then he put his hands atop his head and closed his eyes.

"I think I staved it off," he said.

"I said be quiet," said John.

"Just so you know, there is one thing that *is* against the law and that's lootin' a house fire."

John peered out again, waiting for his moment.

"Consider yourself forewarned," said Billy Ray. He peered, too, from his end of the car. "Damn if that ain't some hellfire and brimstone, though. Ain't smelled anything like it in my life. I imagine that's what the asshole of Evil smells like."

He got no reply. John had already slipped away.

IV

John ducked behind trees and cars, crawling on all fours through the neighboring side yard. The apartment building was brick and therefore the edifice remained, though great black smudges of ash ringed the windows. He got to one of the side windows and looked into what used to be Professor H's living room.

All of what he could see was a grotesque blackness, shiny and still dripping from the fire-hose drenching. Nothing could have survived inside. Still he wanted to see it for himself. This ruined, burned out place would reveal where to go next. He made sure no one was watching him, and then he climbed in through the black hole.

His foot crunched carbonized debris: glass, plaster, what was once a fine Persian rug. He headed for the hallway, but there it was even darker. He went all the way to the bedroom, hoping to find something. Some marker, a sense of direction. It was all a black maw. He doubled back to the bathroom. The charred clawfoot tub. No more shiny pink robe behind the door.

Then he found the kitchen. In the dark, at the table, some-one sat. Like he was waiting for supper to be served. This was just a dream or else John had at last come to understand that nothing in his natural born days was anything but a dream. There was no special alarm about a man sitting at a burned-out kitchen table. And not just a man. This was his faceless father. Waiting for him to come. As it had been ordained since before everything had started. The man with the ruined face stood. He was calm. This is where he was meant to be. This is what he was meant to do. All along. In his arms, he held a small black dog. The dog slept, the rhythmic in and out of its small ribcage. He carried the living thing to his son in the dark.

V

Billy Ray sat with his back propped up against the same parked car, his eyes now closed. Just under his breath, he hummed "Blessed Be the Ties that Bind." Virginia lay on her side with her back to Billy Ray. Her chest rose and fell in an easy, peaceful rhythm. Billy Ray could not have known it, but she was awake. She was staring at the broken tile of sidewalk just in front of her. When she felt something nudging at her neck, she shuffled herself a small distance away from the contact. It nudged again and then it whined. She turned and found a quivering black mass. A sooty little dog. Edward inched closer to her and she picked him up. John rejoined them, covered in soot and out of breath.

"Look what I found," Virginia said.

Billy Ray opened one eye to see what had roused her. He sized things up and closed the eye again.

"I don't care what you do or how much you cry," he said, "that thing ain't sleeping in the house."

VI

They did not head back in the direction from which they had come. They kept going, not yet thinking of a destination or how they would put their heads on pillows in beds under a familiar roof. Virginia held onto Edward like he was her own small child. A train sounded off in the distance, a low, throaty chant. A track ran through this neighborhood, too, just on the other side of the row of houses across the street. Now they proceeded down the sidewalk single file, Billy Ray in the rear. Edward bobbed along with his chin resting on Virginia's shoulder.

"You know the worst of it?" said Billy Ray. "I pretty much lost my whole damn buzz."

"I'm still not talking to you," said Virginia.

"I didn't say you were," said Billy Ray.

"Long as you know," she said.

"This too shall pass," he said.

"Maybe," she said.

"O ye of little faith," he said. "When has it ever not?"

A whiny buzz behind them built. Billy Ray was the first to hear it. The pinprick headlight bobbed down the street. As it got closer, it swerved onto the sidewalk and headed right at him.

"Something wicked this way comes," he muttered.

Karl's weapon in this instance was a greasy bicycle chain. He swung it over his head like a lasso. By the time Billy Ray could make out what it was, the chain lashed across his face and he crumpled on the walk, his hands clutching his mouth.

As he passed, Karl took a swipe at Virginia but John grabbed her and dove out of the way. Karl zipped his moped past and swung back around, a bizarre Black Knight in a modern-day joust.

John yanked Virginia up and they scurried between two houses, toward the tracks and the thin row of trees and vines at the property line in back of the houses. Now the train whistle was louder, and John could feel the enormous weight of the strung together metal cars. He pulled Virginia along as she clutched Edward close to her chest. They had a window. Karl had not seen them duck away. They could, like bandits, hop the train and escape. The big, slow thing lumbered past. Real thunder rumbled and it started to rain. John let go of Virginia and jogged along the track, trying to time his jump into the first open freight car. Once he climbed in, he would pull Virginia up with him.

"What about Billy?" she shouted.

But the beady little headlight found them. Karl's moped appeared at the opening between the two houses and headed toward them.

John dashed back and grabbed Virginia's hand, then started running next to the train. It was picking up pace and soon it would be too fast for them to hop. He let go of Virginia again and grabbed on to the car, feeling its immense pull. After he climbed in, he reached down to Virginia who had no choice but to run alongside the train herself. Still, she hesitated before reaching for him to pull her up.

When she did her hand slipped. It was pouring now. Water falling in sheets.

The thin, sawing whir of the scooter drew closer.

They tried again. This time John grabbed her free arm with both hands and pulled with all he had. She and Edward slid into the car with him. Karl zoomed alongside the train and shouted above the noise.

"Did you think I would just forget?" he screamed. "Is that what you thought? You done shit where I eat not once but twice now. I will fucking find you, don't you worry goddammit—"

The train picked up still more speed. Karl slowed the scooter and turned away, down an alley and off into the night.

VII

"We have to go back," said Virginia. She was soaked and sobbing, near the edge of the car. "We can't just leave him there. Who knows what that evil man is going to do to him."

"We'll have to wait until the train slows down," said John. The houses sped past in a single stream.

"No—now!"

Virginia jumped up and made for the opening, but John intercepted her. She fought him and then she let him hold onto her. Outside, a quickening blur of houses. An undulating sea of kudzu vine. A plan had been forming in his mind. For a split second it had all been clear to him. When he had pulled Virginia up onto the train with him, it seemed possible for them to ride away together. Away from all the things chasing them, from all the ill-advised attachments they had made. It was a life they could leave behind for something else. Something peaceful and serene. But Virginia's face—fierce, determined—told him that was just a dream.

"Give me a second," he said, "and then we'll jump off."

He scooped up Edward, who had wandered to sniff out the corners of the freight car. John put the little dog in his backpack and zipped it up. He looped it tight around both shoulders so that he could have both arms free to cushion his fall, then he took Virginia's hand.

"I'm going to count," he said. "When I get to three, we go."

She nodded quickly and eyed the kudzu.

"One," said John.

The train sounded a loud whistle.

"Two."

The rain slowed. In protest, Edward yipped and pawed the edges of his tight quarters. Before John could finish the count-down, Virginia pulled him toward the door and, together, they leapt.

VIII

John lay face down in the thick blanket of vines surrounded by silence. At first he was without all the other senses, too, but then they returned one at a time. The smell of the wet soil. A dark, funky smell. Something like the essential oils in a wild animal's thick coat. Then he could feel that his elbow had been scraped open and there was dirt and grit in it. Droplets of dissipating rain beat against the wide drum of his back. Both of his fists were full of wet, green leaves. Below him lived a universe of insects, underground rivers, dark matter, magma. These were the useless truths that came to him in the slow silence after his leap with Virginia from the train.

Then he was aware that his glasses were not on his face. He pushed up on all fours. Colors and shapes blended, the version of semi-blindness that had been familiar to him for as long as he could remember. He reached out to either side of him, groping for the heavy horn-rims. No immediate luck. He felt movement ten feet to his right, so he dropped his search for sight and went to the source of the motion.

Virginia was on her back, propped up on her elbows, her head leaned back and she was gasping for air. She could not find anywhere near enough of it to fill her lungs. It looked like she was giving birth. Raindrops hit her face. One dove into her open mouth, and then another. Something gave and her lungs filled up with a loud rushing sound. She rasped and coughed and started once again to cry. As if she had just birthed herself into the world.

"Are you hurt?" John asked.

Virginia nodded her head and kept sobbing.

"Bad?"

She kept nodding.

"Can you walk?"

"My foot," Virginia squeezed out between sobs. "It must be broke."

John crawled closer. "Check the dog," he said.

Virginia inched over to him with some difficulty and fumbled with the backpack still strapped tight to John's back. Edward poked his head out and announced himself with a shrill yap. She pulled the dog out of the backpack and held him close.

"What about you," she asked John. "Are you okay?"

"I can't find my glasses," he said.

Virginia groped around. "They have to be here," she said.

"I've already looked," he said. "Come on. Get on my back. We have to go. I'll carry you. You can be my eyes."

Virginia collected Edward and pulled the backpack from John's back. She put the dog back in it and strapped it over her shoulders, then she climbed onto John. He stood, shaky at first, and started to put one foot in front of the other. In this manner, he carried her piggyback, stumbling blind through the vines and onto the dormant tracks.

IX

Virginia rode on John's back in the direction of Billy Ray. Edward only sometimes fussed as he nestled down at the bottom of the backpack. They looked like they had been in battle, but more than that they looked like one collective thing. A single creature with one set of useful eyes, eight limbs, some that worked better than others, and a squirming hump just beneath its seven-foot shoulders. A strange but somehow formidable conglomeration.

When they reached the place where Karl had downed Billy Ray, neither man was anywhere to be found. There was just dark, soggy turf.

"That man took him," said Virginia. "I know he did."

"Shh. Listen," said John.

They stood quiet in the center of the yard. At first, they could hear only the simple sound of the wind in the trees, water dripping from the branches. Then there came a soft moan in the direction of the bushes in the next yard over. John proceeded with caution toward the sound. Virginia was less cautious.

"Baby, is that you?"

Another moan and a rustle from deep in the bushes.

Virginia again began to cry and, as John got close enough, she jumped down off his back and pogo-hopped on her one good leg. Halfway there, she fell but kept on going, scrambling on her hands and knees into the bushes. His mouth was swollen. His chin, his neck, and the front of his shirt were soaked in dark blood.

"I'm gonna die—please Ginny—don't let me die out here in these people's bushes."

"Hush now. We'll get your mouth fixed up and you'll be good as new."

"That's not it. The sombitch stuck me four times in the guts. I've had it."

Virginia pulled his shirt up to look at his bloody stomach and side. She quit her crying at once. "You won't die," she said. "You can't die. I'm not going to let you."

Billy Ray held up his finger like he was pointing to the sky. "I want one thing. Give me one thing?"

"Yes, baby, anything," said Virginia.

"Marry me. I should have done it like you wanted a long time ago. Let me make you honest."

She wiped her eyes and nose, ready to dismiss it as the delirious rambling of a dying man who was sure he would not have to reckon with the consequences of a rash final act. "There ain't nobody to do it."

Billy Ray aimed his outstretched pointer finger at John.

"He can do it," he said.

Virginia didn't dare look at John.

"It won't count," she said. "It's not legal."

"Laws ain't everything," said Billy Ray. "Not at a time like this."

John made a vestigial push at the bridge of his nose, expecting his lost glasses to be there. He moved in closer to the two of them and got down on one knee. Under the trying circumstances, he did the best he could. The three of them there together on the wet ground, Billy Ray's torn head now in Virginia's lap. John made things up as he went, calling up words and phrases from places faraway in his memory and, even more so, his imagination. Things he had read or seen on TV. He talked about committing thy spirit unto another. About having, holding. Sickness. Health. A grab bag. Most of him did not believe it mattered exactly what he said, or how and why he said it. Most of him believed Billy Ray would give up the ghost right then and there, and then the two of them who were still alive would have to decide how to go and tell someone. But it turned out no one needed to be told. A neighborhood sees and hears even when it does not seem to be watching or listening. Calls had flooded the emergency switchboard. As Billy Ray and Virginia spat out a pair of makeshift I-dos, the flashing lights and sirens asserted themselves upon the scene. Their quick ceremony was over, recorded somewhere in the permanent record. For better or for worse. In health, in certain sickness. Like any true promise, however secret or solemn or small.

The Virgin

This is the story of Faith in Just Outcomes. Young clean Joshua Merriwether has a desire. He pines for a flat-faced girl. The innocent flatness of an herbivorous creature. Something slow and cloven. Flat-faced and long-jawed and simple. He has never heard her say a single word. She attends church on Sunday mornings unadorned. Regardless, young clean Joshua is himself a tongue-tied young man. He himself is no bed of roses. His hair sticks up in the wrong places. It will not sit down. If he went to her, his hair would stick up and he would not have anything to say. He would have nothing worth offering of himself. Thus he offers nothing of himself. After church he walks the long road home having done exactly nothing to abate his pining. The sky is so high and so blue. Boys his age are starting to marry. The flat-faced girl at the church does not say much to any boy of her own accord. A tall boy, however, his face a ruined field of acne, but he is older than either of them and so he is therefore nearabouts a legitimate man—he has taken to sidling next to her in the pew. Even as a younger boy, Joshua did not think he would be anything but an old bachelor. Young clean Joshua walks all the way home with nothing to show for his pining, an empty pit of it building inside him. He walks home with a sliver of a dime in his palm. This dime has come from nowhere or else it is a dime he found on the side of the dusty road. He shoves it in his pocket to hide it away. It is a dime he could have spent on her but that seems like an impossible extravagance. It seems perverse. An act of random intimacy. And that is what it would be. In a matter of weeks she will leave for good with the scarred man who had the nerve to sit next to her in the pew. They will move into the next county, which may as well be a distant nation. It will be the kind of misery that a marriage is. As he ages, Joshua Merriweather hoards everything in his life he's ever earned. His nights are restful and if he has dreams at all, they vanish for good when his eyes flash open to face the simple, solitary day.

Transubstantiation

I

Billy Ray Temple did not die. He was remade. A team of doctors and nurses worked all night to re-route his inner workings. Nothing would ever go in or come out the same way again, but at the end of it, there he was. Living, breathing, mending. The machines, with their blips and beeps, testified to it with an automated insistence that would not be denied. His Momma had been beckoned and she sat in a reclining chair next to her son—blank as always but, as always, there. Present and accounted for. Swollen Billy Ray was strapped in and hooked up to a snarl of tubes and IVs. Accounted for if not quite present. Both of them washed in the pale blue light of a single fluorescent lamp above the head of the bed.

Virginia had her ankle set, casted. John's scrapes were swabbed. There were questions for them, but they gave little in the way of answers. Virginia did not have any, and the ones John could have given would only make his life more difficult than it already was. So he did what he was best at doing: he kept quiet.

John could not see to drive, so Virginia had to manage it. She steered Billy Ray's mother's car, a tank-like Impala, through the backcountry roads. John slept despite himself in the front seat next to her, with Edward curled up in his lap. By the time they got to the trailer, the sky was starting to lighten. John got out and circled around to the driver's side in a blurry daze. He helped Virginia extract herself. Without asking he scooped her up and started to carry her to the door. Edward trotted out of the car and explored, nose to the ground, his new surroundings.

"Put me down," said Virginia. "I've got to learn to get around on my own."

He did as she asked and fished the crutches out of the backseat. He handed them to her, and they limped up to the house together, Edward at their heels. She headed for the back bedroom, making her awkward motion: reach, pull, pause. She knocked the wall and cussed under her breath. When she got to the room and disappeared, Edward gave a guttural whine and scurried after her. John slid face first onto the couch, closed his blind eyes, and started to drift. After a while, he heard the same rhythm from before. Reach, pull, pause. Here and there a knock. Virginia reached the couch and bent down next to his face. Edward hopped up onto the couch and John could here his faint panting.

"You asleep?" she asked.

"Yes," he said.

"Will you come back in the bed with me?"

John opened one eye.

"I don't mean it that way," she said. "I don't make promises like what I did with Billy Ray and not keep it. Not now. I love him. I do. I just want someone next to me."

"What about Edward?" asked John.

"Look at him," she said. "He wants you back there too."

They both lay on their backs in Billy Ray and Virginia's bed, Virginia now tucked under John's arm and Edward burrowed in between them. The sun was rising and the room was filling up with warm light. They were both dirty and bruised from the night, both half asleep but unable to drift completely away.

"You mad I lied?" she asked.

"About what?"

"Me and Billy Ray," she said. "Us being married."

"That's not a lie. It was more true than not," he said. "Now it's all true anyway."

"It's like I said before," she said. She opened her eyes and raised her head to look at him. "It's just always been him. I can't explain it."

She closed her eyes again and dropped her head against his chest.

"You don't mind it though?" he said. "He's so broken now."

They started to succumb to sleep.

"You mean moving his bowels into a bag?" she asked.

"All of it," said John. "I mean all of it."

"That doesn't bother me," said Virginia "I've got a soft spot for tortured souls."

Edward flinched and gave voice to a strange sound: part whimper, part muted bark from down deep in his gullet. The early stages of a dog's restless sleep.

Virginia spoke again, her voice trailing off. "I think the time's coming," she said, "when we might have to bust up this threesome. Foursome, now, I guess."

"I know," said John.

"Not yet though."

"No," he said, "not yet."

And then they slept. Edward, as if he knew that someone should keep a vigil, stirred awake. He stood and circled once. He plopped back down but kept his head raised, like some better angel of their collective nature, watching over them.

II

The unified vision came soon after John fell asleep. It was all of these things at once, in no order: the face of a sad woman who may or may not have been his mother worrying her hands together; a hawk skimming the manmade lake; the classroom where he burned his palm; the sun setting behind a Martin house in a green field; the dumpster where he was discovered by the mean, workaday world; vines growing around his broken horn-rimmed glasses; a vim and vigorous Billy Ray preaching on a wide stage, a great choir of boys behind him; Virginia's beatific face smiling up at him in the backseat of the Pinto; the decrepit shed of his childhood; the empty Duckworthy shower, a nozzle dripping; a sleek, smooth leg; a fetus in a womb; a plate of eggs and grits and bacon; a pile of black ash that then formed itself into a plucky little dog; a syringe pulling in a drop of blood and then injecting its contents into a vein; a pink newborn; slick lip gloss applied to a full, soft bottom lip; Edward old and tired and full of sighs, waiting patiently for the end; Karl sitting in the driver's seat of the Pinto, a leering, smug smile on his face; the still surface of the manmade lake at night.

This was the life he had lived so far, the life that was to come. All of it appropriately jumbled. No proof that it meant something. He could not then parse out what he saw. But he saw it and he knew that he had seen it. What he had seen had called him out.

John opened his eyes and stirred Virginia. She was dead asleep and it took some persistence. They had been sleeping for a long time and it was now afternoon. When she woke, she was groggy and the room was hot.

"What, baby," she said. "I'm sleeping."

"I know what to do," he said. "But I need your help."

Virginia opened her eyes and realized John was not who she thought he was at first. Edward rustled in between them and it came back to her. For a second she had lost her place, but now she remembered. This was not how it looked. Everything had changed.

"With what?" she said. "I can't do much laid up like this."

John walked over to the mirror on the wall. He spoke to himself as much as he did to her.

"I wonder if there is such a thing as a pretty lie."

III

Anyone can wear a painted mask. Transformation is something else. An unearthing of what is already there, somewhere. There is no lie in it. It is exactly the opposite.

John ran the hot water and stepped into the tub. He sudsed the soap in his hands and started to wash the dirt off his body. He began at his feet, lifting them out of the water, first the right and then the left. Fingering his toes and the places in between them, then the arches and his heels. He moved up past one ankle, over the long, narrow shin bone and around to the rounded meaty muscle behind it. He went back to the soap dish and lathered again, then stood up so that he could proceed to the top half of his leg and in towards the groin. When he reached his genitals, he thought of how, when his mother bathed him as a child, she called that part of him his delicates. Even then that seemed strange to him. Only under specific circumstances were they anything like delicate. Mostly they were ropy and elastic, as they were now. He washed them with no special reverence and moved on to the rest of his body. The long, flat stomach ridged almost imperceptibly with muscle. His arms and neck, his smooth chest, his hard, delineated ribcage. He reached around himself and managed the best he could on his back, and then he sat in the warm, soapy water. He lathered up his long black hair with a palm full of pearl-colored shampoo. When he was clean, he sunk down in the tub and lay still in the water. It smelled good and clean but it was a gray-brown color from all the dirt and sweat and dried up rainwater he had just scrubbed off himself. He popped the stopper and let the fluid drain down, listening to its familiar sucking sound. When the soily water was gone, he turned on the shower and rinsed himself, lingering in the warm stream until it turned lukewarm and then cold. He dried off, shivering but invigorated by the tail end of his elaborate ablution, and he wrapped the towel around his waist. He found a razor and a can of shaving cream. At the sink, he shaved his face and neck as close as he could, running the razor first in one direction and then, very slowly and pulling his skin tight with his free hand, in the opposite one. When he had finished with all the preparations he could be expected to know how to do, he went into the bedroom and presented himself to Virginia. She had agreed to help him with the rest.

"You're sure?" she asked him. She was lying on the bed, her back propped up by pillows, as she rubbed the blissful Edward's belly.

"Never more," he said.

"Okay then," she said. "This ought to be interesting."

And so, with John as clean as he could be from head to toe, they began to make him into something else. This required intuition, artistry, harsh chemicals. Calcium thioglycolate to remove the body hair on parts of him that would be exposed. Hydrogen peroxide, ammonia and isopropyl alcohol to turn the hair on his head from black to a rich russet color.

"Is that the way it's supposed to smell?" John asked.

"What do you want it to smell like?" said Virginia. "Nobody ever said all this was sweetness and light."

She washed out the dye and towel dried his hair, then she sat him in a chair by the sink and styled it, pulling at it with a brush while she fluffed it with a hair dryer. Then she set about preparing his face: moisturizer, an ultra light base to match his coloring. Then a discreet application of mascara, eyeliner, lip liner, gloss. All of it clean and clear as it could be, to emphasize the smooth texture of his skin, the underlying symmetry of his bones. When she was through, they both stared into the mirror. John strained his eyes. He could barely see the face she'd found in him.

"Does it look right?" he said. He leaned forward to get a closer look. "It has to look natural."

"You're a pretty girl, if that's what you mean," she said. "Mostly there's not anything natural about it. You asked me before if I believe in pretty lies. The answer to that is yes I do. Pretty mostly *is* a lie."

Then she blew him a kiss and went to the closet to find him something to wear that would show off his pretty, round backside.

IV

"Trick-or-treat?" said John.

Virginia turned off the television and stood to get a better look at him. John took a few tentative steps toward her, stumbling in the heels she had laid out for him to wear. He caught himself just before he fell and decided it was safer if he stood where he was.

"Say something," he said. "You're making me feel stupid."

"No," she said, "no. It's just. I don't know." She started to grin. "You remember when you said I had the prettiest everything?"

"Yeah," he said.

"You give me a run for my money," she said.

John cast his eyes down to the ground and he smiled a little bit at his feet, unable to decide whether he should be embarrassed or proud. He changed the subject instead.

"You sure you're up for driving me?"

"What are you gonna do?" said Virginia. "Walk?"

"You're right," said John. "I need you to teach me before I go."

"I'm the one with the broken foot," she said.

"Just watch me and tell me what I'm doing wrong."

"Come closer," she said.

He did and she inspected his feet from over the edge of the couch.

"Tighten those straps first. That's part of the problem."

John leaned up against the couch and did as she told him.

"Walk down the hall."

John walked, plopping his entire foot down at once in a mannish, straight-hipped lunge.

"No," said Virginia. "That's wrong. Let your heel hit first and take shorter steps. And you have to swivel your hips some."

John put all of it into his head at once and overcompensated, taking mincing steps and swiveling his hips like he was made of tin. This, of course, made Virginia laugh.

"What's so funny?" he said.

"What's *not* funny?" she said. "At least you're cute."

John was frustrated but he started again.

"Don't bend your knees so much."

"It's too much to remember all at once," he said.

"Welcome to womanhood," she said. "Just keep trying. Heel first. Straight out in front of you. Like a feline."

"Feline?" he said, hobbling along without much improvement.

"Women have more in common with cats than they do men," said Virginia. "A cat moves every part of its body when it walks."

John kept practicing, his arms held out a little to his sides like a tightrope walker.

"And cats are graceful and clean and picky about what they eat," said Virginia. "Plus they'd have you believe they don't ever take a poop at all when really most of us do it at least half again as much as a man. We're just a lot quicker about it."

"Now you're playing with me," said John. He reached the end of the hallway and turned around.

"Not one bit," she said.

He tried again. Better this time. He walked toward her with a sense of purpose, pivoted sharply, then headed back down the hall. It was passable. Maybe better than passable.

"Now give your tail a little twitch," she called after him. "Just for show."

He complied and she whooped and clasped her hands together. Edward barked at the commotion and the strange new version of John slinking down the hallway.

V

The old man Mose was used to seeing unusual things. He was not afraid of them. He invited them. What's more, he knew when they were preparing to reveal themselves to him. As he walked down the tracks, back home from a day of wandering out in the sticky-hot world, he felt the familiar gooseflesh rising on his neck. When he was a younger man, this would have quickened his breath. He would have been worried about what he was going to have to see, whether he would be able to take it in without betraying himself to the world of solid things. As he got older, he took the position that there was no such thing as a world of solid things. Or at least there was no difference between it and all the other worlds he saw.

Even then, in the glare of the late afternoon sun, he had to blink, then blink again, to be sure of what he saw up in the middle distance. A barefoot woman carried another woman out the door of the Temple trailer by the tracks. The carried woman—the young Reverend's live-in lady friend—she carried things herself: a pair of crutches and a little dog. The barefoot woman put the other woman down once they had navigated the steps, then she put on a pair of heels and took the dog while the other one propped herself up with the crutches. The two of them took great pains to get themselves in the car, and so they did not see him. As they drove away, he rested on his walking stick for a long time, the gooseflesh slowly dissipating. He clucked his tongue and kept on his way, ducking back into the woods, assured now that something even stranger was on its way.

VI

"Don't go left up here," said John. "Go right."

The bright red sun was in Virginia's face and she was fighting with the driver's side visor. She had given John her oversized sunglasses. They were the fashion with the young ladies of the day, but they also shielded his telltale eyes.

"Right?" she said. "There ain't nothing that way. I thought you wanted to go into town."

"I know there's nothing that way," said John. He avoiding looking at her and stared out his side window instead. "And we are going into town. We have some stops to make first."

VII

They drove out into the green nothing. A make-believe land of vine-choked hollows and shadowy ravines shrouding the dark red earth. For a full twenty minutes they went without seeing a living thing, no birds or cows or ribsy dogs. Navigation was easy enough. Stay straight. There was nowhere to turn.

When they came to a gravel side road, John told Virginia this was where he wanted to go. The big car was a tight fit and the road was poor. There were dense woods to either side of them and still no sign of life. Then, here and there, they started to see evidence of human habitation. A mailbox next to a narrow drive leading back into the woods. And another and then, in time, another. They cleared a bend in the road and drove up a little hill, at the top of which was another rusted out old mailbox with a name painted on it in white letters.

"Slow down," said John. "This is it."

Virginia stopped the car in front of the mailbox.

"You know somebody named Crowe?"

John stared at the box a long time, like it might get up and walk away. "Maybe," he said. "I don't know. We'll see."

———

The driveway was too narrow and overgrown. Halfway down, Virginia had to stop the car. John took off his high-heeled shoes and got out. Virginia got out too, but only to call after him.

"You know I can't make it back there with my foot like this."

John kept walking, stepping over a fallen tree limb.

"Stay with Edward," he said. "I won't be long."

"You think it's a good idea to present yourself to somebody you haven't seen in a while all decked out like you are?"

"No," he said. And he kept walking down the gravel drive until she could not see him anymore.

Soon enough the ramshackle white house presented itself. Its concrete stoop and the broken swing. The numbers his mother had painted on the doorframe in blue paint were more artful than he had remembered. The old window unit was on, wheezing like it always had, even though the door was halfway open, the old useless screen letting in the big, biting flies. John crossed the yard like a boy coming home from school.

He knocked on the screen but there was no answer from inside the house, so he walked in uninvited. The olfactory sense is the one linked closest to memory, and a stream of times past entered him through his nostrils. Like smelling salts. The thick smell of poisoned rats, stiff and decomposing underneath the house, in the walls. The fresh dung of those still alive. Wood rot. The mildewed armchair in the corner where his mother used to sit. When he was young, these smells promised that any number of dark things could happen, and there was nothing and no one to save him but himself.

The house itself was small. One level, two bedrooms. The front door opened into the living room. The furniture even then was spare but now the room was nearly empty. Some things had to be removed, soaked through as they were with the blood and other fluids that had once coursed through his father's mad brain. John went back further into the house, checked the bedroom where he had slept. The walls were bare, painted over. Gone were the markings he had made there. He went to the bathroom, the kitchen. All were much the same as they had been—dusty, dirty, lacking comforts, like a den of near animals. And all were empty. He knew, then, where she was.

There was a door off the kitchen and it led to a dank back porch. When he was a boy, his mother would retreat there. As he got older, she would take a small jelly jar full of beer with a thin rime of chopped ice bobbing at the rim. Sometimes John would sit out there with her and watch the bubbles in the beer as they tried in vain to burst through the frozen surface. She stayed out there longer and longer, and as the afternoon turned to evening, she started refilling the little jar again and again until she had no choice but to start on supper before her husband came home.

John walked with his bare feet into the filthy kitchen. Rat pellets dotted the surface of the stove. All the cabinet doors were gone, and the vermin had made a mess chewing holes through ancient boxes of oats and grains and white flour. There was a wide hole rotted through the linoleum in the floor, and he could see through to the dirt in the crawlspace. The place was a ruin of a ruin. He opened the door to the porch to find his mother.

She was there, as he expected her to be. She too was ruined, but he had already born witness to that during the days he lived there. She still looked older than she was. Her hair was matted and thin, and too much of her bones showed. This was all as he had remembered. She sat on a white plastic chair he did not remember. Something, at least, was new. She held her little jar of beer on her knee and stared out at the grove of trees behind the house. There was a honeysuckle bush, too—the white flowers set against the deep, untouched green out back. A bee-loud glade. She was lost in that unspectacular pleasure. She did not notice the door open. When John touched her shoulder to announce himself, it jolted her.

"My goodness," she said. Her speech was slow and her eyes were wide. "I—I can't say I'm prepared for no company." She leaned back away from John but her eyes, bleary from the beer, searched his face. She started to shake her head. "Child, who are you? You must be lost."

"I'm not lost, Momma," said John. "I used to live here."

"You here about renting the place?" she said. "Because I'm not renting it out. I live here."

He walked past her, down the porch steps and surveyed the green backyard.

"Anyhow," she said, "before you know it the coloreds come in and I don't want to rent to no coloreds."

"The shed's not here anymore," he said.

"I don't know who you are or why you're here," said his mother. "I want you to leave now."

"What happened to that old shed, Momma? It used to be right over there but it's gone."

The woman shut her mouth tight and kept silent for a long time. John walked back up onto the porch to get away from a nasty cloud of mosquitoes. He stood directly in front of his mother, as close as he dared. She craned her neck up at him.

"I never had no daughter," she said. "That's how I know you're lost."

John took off his sunglasses and bent down so that his face was closer to hers. He could hear the tinkle of the ice in her jelly jar. The vantage point and the smell of the beer forced him further back into his youth. The only times when he felt even a little bit safe. Out there, the two of them silent as the birdless trees.

"Did you ever have a son?"

Her mouth was open and he could smell her breath. The smell of neglected teeth, badly mixed up insides. She brought the jar to her lap and, cupping it in both hands, she stared down into it. She must have found something there because when she looked up, her eyes flashed and her mouth tightened.

"No," she said. "I never had no husband neither."

John stayed bent in front of her for a moment longer, like some kind of supplicant, then he stood to leave.

"I guess you're right, then," he said. "I guess I am lost."

When John got to the car, Virginia spoke to him but he could not hear her. The things that she was asking him to tell her— had he found who he was looking for, did they recognize him, what did they say about the way he looked—did not need any answers. The only question worth answering after his home- coming was this: was he free of it? And the answer was yes. He was as free as a man who had never been born at all.

VIII

There was one other stop to make. Virginia resisted when he told her where he needed to go, but he was so silent, so resolute, she had no choice but to relent and take him there.

"I won't get out of the car," she said. "I can tell you that right now."

They retraced their route, back in the direction of civilization. The brand of civilization that they knew. Just outside the town limits, they came to a subdivision of tidy little squared-off houses, and Virginia turned in. They wound back through the curves, past the neatly edged yards, the wide sidewalks, the CHILDREN AT PLAY signage. A man with thinning hair and knobby knees walked a fat hound dog. He waved at them, like they belonged. Virginia steered into a cul de sac and sidled the car up to the bright white curb. She kept the car running.

"His real name's Souksavath," she said. "You call him something else, they won't know who you're talking about."

John pressed the little white button on the door frame, and it sounded inside the house. A small Asian woman appeared, pretty and ageless and unadorned. Her face was wide, her nose a small button, and her dark eyes were alert and questioning.

"Can I see Souk—" John stumbled on the word.

"Souksavath?" the woman asked, and John nodded. She closed the door softly. Behind it he heard her call out in a torrent of language he had never heard before. Her voice faded as she moved away from the door, and then he heard bounding footfalls ascending from the lower level of the house and up towards the foyer.

The door opened just enough for Chewie to poke his head out.

"Do I know you, fair maiden?" he asked.

"We met through Billy Ray," said John. "You pulled me out of the river the other night."

Chewie opened the door a little wider and he moved in toward John to get a closer look.

"Damn. Shapeshifter," he said. "You always wear the coolest specs."

"I came to tell you where to find the materials I showed you," said John.

Chewie shot a glance up the steps behind him and scooted out the door.

"Whoa now," he whispered, "loose lips sink ships. Mi madre es Laotian—Laotian women can hear everything. That's their superpower."

John handed Chewie a folded piece of paper. "We buried it," he said. "Out by the Mounds. I drew a map, the best I could. It's yours if you want it."

Chewie pushed the paper back at John. "I said I don't want anything to do with it. Karl knows all, Karl sees all, and Karl is a mean motherfucker. Those are just the circumstances."

John grabbed Chewie's hand and slapped the paper into it, and then he walked back to the running car without turning around. "Take it," he said. "In case the circumstances change."

IX

Virginia drove with Edward in her lap. John, in the passenger's seat, wore the large amber-tinted sunglasses even though the sun had nearly set. In the distance, as they got near town, a single landmark loomed over what was otherwise a landscape of trees. It was the white bowl of the college football stadium. This was a structure John knew well from his days wandering the town, waiting for the nights with Karl and his stable of sad men. The mass of white concrete had worked itself into the neighborhood, growing slowly over time. Even though it was made of different stuff from its surroundings, it had always seemed like it belonged right where it was. But from this distance, seen anew, it seemed large and incongruous with the landscape, like some hulking alien ship that had just arrived. John felt like he belonged to such a ship, like he had begun an inevitable journey back to it. John knew firsthand that a large cemetery sat across the street from the stadium, and a hamburger and hot dog stand did a lively business in its shadows. He had frequented both; the latter for obvious reasons, the former because it was a place where he could be as quiet as he wanted without feeling self-conscious.

"Remember now: the right way to talk isn't high as much as it is soft," Virginia said. "A lot of men like a little husk in a girl's voice."

John nodded and inspected the red lacquered surface of his fingernails.

"Better yet," said Virginia, "don't talk at all, if you can help it. Most men like that even better."

The streetlights flickered and buzzed as they labored to come alive for the evening. Here and there, the young people traveled in groups of three and four, ready for loud music and alcohol and the impossible promise of sex. It was all familiar to him, but it felt like he had been gone years, not days. Nothing about him was the same.

The car came to a halt a safe distance from the convenience store. John reached for the door without saying anything to Virginia, but she grabbed his arm.

"You sure you want do this?" she asked.

"This is the way I saw it," he said.

"Sometimes a dream is just a dream. I've never had one that wasn't."

"It's supposed to be this way," said John. "I've got to deal with him sooner or later. Best it's on my terms."

Virginia leaned back in the seat. She scratched her head and sighed, then rested both hands on top of the steering wheel.

"I can't say I don't want him to come to *somebody's* terms," she said. "You have to promise you'll be careful. I can't have something happen to you too. Something worse."

John gave her a half-hearted smile.

"You can't even see to begin with and now you got those damn sunglasses on. How will you know where you're going? It's dark."

"There's not much about this I want to see," he said. He pushed the door open and got out of the car. Before he left, he leaned back into the car.

"Oh sweet Jesus," she said. "Don't even say it. I know you're going to try to thank me. I just hope you don't have to forgive me instead. Because I won't forgive myself if something happens to you."

"Consider yourself forgiven," he said. He leaned in even closer and kissed her on the forehead, and then he left for good. A smudge of lip gloss on her forehead. An Ash Wednesday thumbprint in her own shimmery pink cosmetics.

III

Man

—*noun*

1. A human being; — opposed to *beast*.

These **men** went about wide, and **man** found they none, But fair country, and wild beast many [a] one. *R. of Glouc.*
The king is but a **man**, as I am; the violet smells to him as it doth to me. *Shak.*
<—" 'Tain't a fit night out for man nor beast! " [W.C. Fields] —>

2. Especially: An adult male person; a grown-up male person, as distinguished from a woman or a child.

When I became a **man**, I put away childish things. *I Cor. xiii. 11.*
Ceneus, a woman once, and once a **man**. *Dryden.*

3. The human race; mankind.

And God said, Let us make **man** in our image, after our likeness, and let them have dominion. *Gen. i. 26.*
The proper study of mankind is **man**. *Pope.*

4. The male portion of the human race.

Woman has, in general, much stronger propensity than **man** to the discharge of parental duties. *Cowper.*

5. One possessing in a high degree the distinctive qualities of manhood; one having manly excellence of any kind. *Shak.*

This was the noblest Roman of them all . . . the elements So mixed in him that Nature might stand up And say to all the world This was a **man**! *Shak.*

6. An adult male servant; also, a vassal; a subject.

Like master, like **man**. *Old Proverb.*
The vassal, or tenant, kneeling, ungirt, uncovered, and holding up his hands between those of his lord, professed that he did become his **man** from that day forth, of life, limb, and earthly honor. *Blackstone.*

7. A term of familiar address often implying on the part of the speaker some degree of authority, impatience, or haste; as, Come, *man*, we 've no time to lose !

8. A married man; a husband; — correlative to *wife*.

I pronounce that they are **man** and wife. *Book of Com. Prayer.*
every wife ought to answer for her **man**. *Addison.*

9. One, or any one, indefinitely; — a modified survival of the Saxon use of *man*, or *mon*, as an indefinite pronoun.

A **man** can not make him laugh. *Shak.*
A **man** would expect to find some antiquities; but all they have to show of this nature is an old rostrum of a Roman ship. *Addison.*

10. One of the piece with which certain games, as chess or draughts, are played. &hand; *Man* is often used as a prefix in composition, or as a separate adjective, its sense being usually self-explaining; as, *man* child, *man* eater or *man*eater, *man*-eating, *man* hater or *man*hater, *man*-hating, *man*hunter, *man*-hunting, *man*killer, *man*-killing, *man* midwife, *man* pleaser, *man* servant, *man*-shaped, *man*slayer, *man*stealer, *man*-stealing, *man*thief, *man* worship, etc. *Man* is also used as a suffix to denote a person of the male sex having a business which pertains to the thing spoken of in the qualifying part of the compound; ash*man*, but-ter*man*, laundry*man*, lumber*man*, milk*man*, fire*man*, show*man*, water*man*, wood*man*. Where the combination is not familiar, or where some specific meaning of the compound is to be avoided, *man* is used as a separate substantive in the foregoing sense; as, apple *man*, cloth *man*, coal *man*, hardware *man*, wood *man* (as distinguished from wood*man*). Man ape (Zoöl.), a anthropoid ape, as the gorilla. — Man at arms, a designation of the fourteenth and fifteenth centuries for a soldier fully armed. — Man engine, a mechanical lift for raising or lowering people through considerable distances; specifically (Mining), a contrivance by which miners ascend or descend in a shaft. It consists of a series of

landings in the shaft and an equal number of shelves on a verti-
cal rod which has an up and down motion equal to the distance
between the successive landings. A man steps from a landing to
a shelf and is lifted or lowered to the next landing, upon which
he them steps, and so on, traveling by successive stages. — Man
Friday, a person wholly subservient to the will of another, like
Robinson Crusoe's servant Friday. — Man of straw, a puppet;
one who is controlled by others; also, one who is not respon-
sible pecuniarily. — Man-of-the earth (Bot.), a twining plant
(Ipomœa pandurata) with leaves and flowers much like those
of the morning-glory, but having an immense tuberous fari-
naceous root. — Man of war. (a) A warrior; a soldier. *Shak.* (b)
(Naut.) See in the Vocabulary. — To be one's own man, to have
command of one's self; not to be subject to another.

[Fig. #56. Stick figure. No defining characteristics. Two plain
dots for eyes, a flatline for a mouth. The rest of the page is
blank, asking to be filled.]

A Harrowing

I

A pregnant woman and her strung-out boyfriend stood near the front of the store, considering an aisle's worth of candy and confections. The boyfriend turned his attention to the clanging glass door. He was unabashed, his eyes moving up and down the image he saw. The woman he was with felt his absence and pulled her own gaze off the Now & Laters. When she saw what he was seeing, she punched him hard in the arm.

"You think I don't see you checking her out?" she said, loud enough for the whole store to hear. "I'm right fucking here. Jesus."

The skinny man rubbed his arm and cast his eyes to the floor.

"I don't know what you got your panties in a wad about," he said. "Men look. That's biology."

"You don't know shit about school subjects," she said, and she hit him again, this time harder and square in the chest. She gave up her candy search and stormed, cursing, to another part of the store. He rubbed his chest and followed her, cursing too.

Karl sat on a tall stool with his back to the rest of the store and its minor commotion, and though a young woman hovered at the counter behind him, he continued with what he was working on, fabricating an inventory form. She gave a polite, throat-clearing cough, but Karl did not look up from his crucial form.

"In a minute," he grumbled.

This was followed by another soft cough.

"Which part of 'in a minute' don't you fucking understand—" and then he registered what he saw. It was a young woman in a sundress. He could not see her eyes behind her wide sunglasses, but the rest of her was quite enough. She smiled—a dimple; straight, white teeth. The relentless symmetry of an imperceptible nose, mouth a Cupid's bow, the sculptural grace and logic of her well-formed jaw and cheekbones. Karl leaned back against the counter he had been working on and tried, with mixed results, to muster a charming grin.

"I'm sorry to interrupt your paperwork," she said. "That must be important."

"Never more important than the customer right there in front of you," he said. "That there's straight out of the corporate literature."

Karl sauntered over to her, placing both his hands on the counter in the unmistakable gesture of a mating ritual: this was his territory and he claimed it.

"Customer service is the lifeblood of this business," he said. "I am here for you and you alone."

"I'd like a pack of cigarettes," she said, "and I'll be out of your way."

"No hurry," said Karl. "What flavor?"

She pointed over his left shoulder. "Those menthols, please."

"A sweet cigarette for a sweet young lady," said Karl. He reached up to retrieve the smokes and placed them on the counter. She unwrapped the pack right there and took out a cigarette, then handed Karl the cellophane.

"I'm sorry to say you can't smoke in this here shithole. Sets off the sprinkler and the fire marshal comes."

She pushed out her lip into what was a conspicuous and comely pout. "I don't have a light," she said. "I was hoping I could get one from you."

Karl's face registered a brief note of surprise, but he recovered just as quickly.

"I'll tell you what," he said. "I can do you one better than that. I run the show here, and I can close her up whenever I want. You give me five minutes, I'll give you a light. A ride. Stronger smoke. Whatever you need and then some."

"You are a very confident person," she said.

"I just live in the moment, is all," he said. "That's my secret."

She put the unlit cigarette back in the pack and smiled. Up and down, she took his measure. Then she grabbed the pack of cigarettes and started for the door.

"Five minutes?" she said.

"Five minutes," said Karl.

Her smile widened and she gave him a slow, confident nod. "I'll be outside," she said.

II

The lights flicked off inside the store one by one. The pregnant woman and her boyfriend left the store eating their packaged ice creams. He goosed her on the way, as a means of reconciliation, and she squealed. They both laughed and hurried off to their week-to-week room in the motel across the street.

Karl emerged from the darkened store with a pilfered case of cheap beer, his head on a swivel. She stood with her back to the brick wall, one leg up under her and the unlit cigarette in her hand. Without a counter between them, all things were now possible. She put the cigarette to her lips. Karl produced a lighter and lit it, and then they walked around to the back alley together. As they turned the corner, Karl put his arm around her narrow waist and let his hand slip down to rest on her firm, round backside. She smoothly reached back and adjusted his hand upward, taking it in hers and threading their fingers together.

"You know where I'm going to take you?" she said.

"Where's that, darling?"

"Only my favorite place in the whole world."

Soon enough the Pinto fired up and headed off in the direction of the lake.

III

They sipped beers and looked out at the lake and up at the stars.

"This place sure is a sight," said Karl.

"Sometimes I think this is as close as I'll ever get to heaven," she said.

"Pretty as you are?" Karl said. "There's a special place in heaven for all the pretty girls like you."

"My mother said handsome is as handsome does," she said.

"Pretty is a whole different ball game," said Karl. "And *you* are pretty."

Karl put his beer on the dash. He reached over and did the same with hers.

"You wear those sunglasses all the time? Must be dark in there."

Karl reached for the sunglasses. She pulled back, took them off herself, slowly, without looking right at him. Karl reached over and turned her chin towards him.

"Good lord," he said. "Them eyes. You need to be showing them things off."

She glanced down and away, uncomfortable with his unblinking way of looking at her.

"No," Karl said. He was stern but also, in his way, soft. "Look at me."

They were face to face, inches apart. The first few drops of an ambivalent rain shower pecked the roof, the windshield. A slow peal of thunder echoed across the wide, flat lake. Karl pulled her toward him and they kissed—soft at first, then more voracious—until, almost tender, he guided her head downward, his fist closing, tightening in her hair.

One Flesh

"And he answered and said unto them, Have ye not read, that he which made them at the beginning made them male and female,
and said,
For this cause shall a man leave father and mother,
and shall cleave to his wife:
and twain shall be one flesh?
Wherefore they are no more twain, but one flesh. What therefore God hath joined together, let not man put asunder."

Asunder

I

When Billy Ray came home to recuperate, he lay in bed all day and all night, a pale, withered version of his former self. His Momma fed him ice-chips like an automaton. Virginia mostly sat on the other side of the bed. She would, when the occasion presented itself, wipe some perspiration from his forehead, which was furled into what seemed to be a permanent row of deep ridges.

On this particular afternoon, Momma was away in the recliner in the front room, taking a rest in front of the television. Virginia sat in the chair where his mother usually sat so that she could face him, and she began to read from the King James Version of the Bible that John had left behind. There were underlined passages, and she picked the ones that spoke best to the concern at hand:

Arise, go thy way: thy faith hath made thee whole.

She flipped a few pages.

I say unto thee, Arise, and take up thy bed and go thy way into thine house.

She flipped again.

Thy faith hath made thee whole; go in peace and be whole of thy plague.

She looked at him like she was waiting for something to happen. He turned his head to the unmanned cup of shavings on the dresser. She leaned over him and grabbed the cup. Spooning a few shavings into his dry mouth, she waited to see if he wanted any more. He closed his eyes and she took this to mean he did not.

"You want me to keep reading?"

Billy Ray closed his eyes tighter and then started shaking his head back and forth, as if to say that the scripture was too bitter a medicine. His eyes popped open wide and he stared straight up at the ceiling. He spoke, but not to Virginia.

"Lord, if you will heal me up—"

He closed his eyes again, beaten down by everything: the burning pain in his middle, the crinkling sound his shit bag made whenever he moved, the soft weight of his unused muscles. Everything. Words were not enough to say all that he meant to say.

But Virginia would not leave it to chance. Even an all-knowing God is best addressed in complete declarative sentences. She grabbed Billy Ray's hand, shut her eyes tight and bowed her head.

"Lord," she said, "if you heal us, we'll be but vessels for your will."

Billy Ray's bottom lip started to quiver like it belonged to a boy with a skinned knee on the playground. He kept his eyes shut tight and then, as a kind of amen, out came a single bold stream of tears.

Almost in answer, there came a firm knock on the front door. It took Momma a few seconds to awaken and gather herself before going to see what it was. When she opened the door, she saw two men, indistinguishable and squat in their square suits and flat-top haircuts. They stood shoulder to shoulder at the threshold, and Momma stared at them without a word.

"We're police officers, ma'am," said one. They both displayed their plasticized identifications.

"We're looking for Miss Justice," said the other.

Momma did not move.

The first investigator spoke again, slower and louder this time. "Is a Virginia Marie Justice on the premises? This is the address we have."

A voice came from behind Momma, followed by a pretty, unadorned face.

"I'm Virginia Justice," she said. Like she had known all along they were coming.

II

The room was gray, windowless. She sat at a plain table across from the same two investigators who had summoned her there. There was a file splayed out in front of one of the investigators. Forms, reports, notebook pages, photographs.

"What are we doing here, Virginia?" said the man with the file. He had fat fingers and, whenever something in the file caught his attention, he tickled the surface of the table like he was playing a very small piano.

"You took the words right out of my mouth," said Virginia. "I don't have the slightest clue what we're doing here."

The other man was standing. He had removed his coat and rolled up his sleeves. He put his hands on the back of the empty chair in front of him and leaned in.

"We expect you might," he said.

Virginia sat with her hands folded in her lap and she giggled despite herself. "You know, I was having trouble telling you two apart. Now you took your coat off for me, so that helps. And you're trying to show your mean streak, and that helps too. He's Good Cop and you're Bad Cop."

Bad Cop flashed a grin.

"This one's a loaded pistol," he said. Good Cop went through the papers in front of him with a stone stoic face.

"If you want to talk about what happened to my husband, I already gave a description of the man who tried to kill him."

Good Cop found something and examined it, speaking without looking up. "Do you know a Karl Adams?"

"I do not."

"We have several eye witnesses that say you probably do," said Bad Cop. He twirled the chair and sat in it backwards. "They say you probably know him well."

Good Cop kept his eyes trained on what he had found in the file.

"A bagger from the IGA out in Hale," he said. "Another three or four from the Bastille bar here in town."

"They all swear they've seen you hop in and out of Mr. Adams's vehicle over the course of the last two weeks," said Bad Cop. He wore an exaggerated smile. As if he had just won an award. "Can't miss it. Orange Ford Pinto. No muffler. You been in a car like that lately?"

"My husband has been in the hospital for the last ten days," she said.

Good Cop tossed what he had in front of her. A photograph of the car. Virginia tried, with some difficulty, to keep her face calm. She was mostly successful. He slid another picture over, this time of the interior. A deep black stain where blood had pooled in the driver's seat.

"We found it out by the lake about a week ago," said Good Cop. He scratched his chin. "You know what we can't find?

Virginia stared straight at him and shrugged, but her jaw had set and she was holding her hands together more tightly.

He took another picture from the pile and showed it to her. A mugshot of Karl from the not-too-distant past. Virginia slapped the table with the flat of her palms.

"That's him that—" but she stopped short.

"That's him that what?" asked Bad Cop. His smile got wider.

She was in it now. Backing out would make it worse. "That's the guy that stabbed my husband," she said.

Good Cop paused, shuffled some papers, reviewed some others. All like he was preparing to file his tax return.

"So then," he looked up at her, "you'd have reason to want him to disappear."

"I have reason to want a lot of things," she said. "That doesn't mean I can make them come to pass."

He went back to sifting through the pile, nodding as if he might be granting her point. He moved on to another line of questions.

"I suggested earlier we can't find Mr. Adams. But that's not entirely true. We did find something that belonged to him."

"Besides the car," said Bad Cop. His smile faded.

"That's right," said Good Cop. "Besides the car." He folded his hands on the table. He was through, for the moment, with the contents of the file. "Have you ever engaged in any sexual activity with Mr. Adams?"

Virginia's eyes narrowed. "I wouldn't come close enough to spit on him."

"Never had relations in the backseat of this vehicle?"

Virginia glared in no particular direction, again trying to swallow any sign of nerves. She had nothing useful to say. She tried to conjure an incredulous laugh but it came out wrong: it was a high squeak that nearly sounded like a young girl's giggle.

Bad Cop tapped his finger on the table and his face fell into a somber mask.

"Somebody goes missing, Miss Justice, and their vehicle turns up with blood all in it," he said, "we're going to give it a good once over. All the science we can muster. You find all manner of things you didn't know you was looking for."

"Stains. Hairs. Fingerprints. Dried fluids," said Good Cop.

"Point is we know *someone* got up close and personal in the backseat of that vehicle, not long before we found it," said Bad Cop. "Hours, maybe days. Maybe more than once."

"We think you might have been a party to it," said Good Cop.

"It's easy enough to find out," said Bad Cop. "Just a swab or two here and there." He gestured in the general direction of her lap.

"I never met that man," said Virginia. "I didn't know him. I was damn sure never intimate with him. In that car or anywhere else. You can swab every hole I got."

The two men exchanged a quick glance.

"And then there's the other thing, of course," said Bad Cop. "The thing we found that used to belong to Mr. Adams."

"You really think we should tell her what we found?"

"I think," said Bad Cop, "she knows damn well what we found."

"It's a real indelicate thing that we found," said Good Cop. "I don't even like to say it, tell the truth."

Bad Cop plastered a smile back on his face. "Something about Miss Justice doesn't strike me as the delicate type."

"I don't know what you're talking about and I don't care what you found."

Good Cop rubbed his eyes and then folded his fat hands back on the table.

"What we found, Miss Justice, was his male member there on the floorboard," he said. "Separated damn near at the base. Maybe bit off, maybe it was cut. We can't tell."

Virginia's eyes got wide and she put her hand to her mouth.

"Clear-cut black widow situation," said Bad Cop. "So to speak."

"Female mates and she kills," said Good Cop. "That's the working theory we got right now."

"Clear-cut," said Bad Cop. "So to speak."

"Now," said Good Cop, "you want to tell us what you did with the rest of him?"

For the Remission of Sins

"Blood is carried away from the heart and through the body in blood vessels called arteries. When an artery has been cut, *bright red* blood issues from the wound in *distinct spurts* or pulses that correspond to the rhythm of the heartbeat. Because the blood in the arteries is under high pressure, quite a large volume of blood can be lost in a short period of time when an artery of significant size is damaged. For this reason, arterial bleeding is considered the most serious type of bleeding; if it is not controlled promptly, it can be fatal."
—*The U.S. Army Survival Manual*

"And he took the cup, and gave thanks, and gave it to them, saying, Drink ye all of it—"

Trial

I

John was filthy and bruised. His hair was matted, the make-up and blood smudged on his face in some strange mask of war. He still wore the sundress, now torn by whatever gauntlets of brush and stumps and rock outcroppings he had wandered through. The heels were long gone and his feet were bloodied and swollen. The front of the dress was a deep brown Rorschach blot of dried humors. Most of it not his own. He huddled by a tree and was examining the ground, cupping his hands and moving them with exaggerated stealth toward something he saw there. Just inches from a patch of decomposing leaves, he snatched. A cricket resisted the tight vice of his right fist. He popped the leggy thing into his mouth and chewed. A snap of exoskeleton and then his mouth and throat filled with what had been inside the thing. Then again he heard footsteps and he pressed on, dizzy and without a sense of where he would go from there.

II

For an indeterminate stretch—days, a week, he was no longer sure when it came to matters of time and place and how
to separate the two—he had traipsed in these dense woods.
More thicket than woods. All day long snagged by thorns and
branches, slipping in mud. Some dark thing had stalked him
all the while, and though he believed he had sometimes caught
glimpses of it, it had not yet made itself known.

The first two nights he did not sleep for the swirl of voices
and visions in his head.

The third night he could not help himself. His body was
spent. He fell into a paralyzed state, dead but not yet dead. His
body imposed a stillness that unencumbered his mind. Free
to do as it pleased, it grew to inhabit the woods entirely. First
the small pocket of space where he lay and then up through the
tall chamber set out by the trees around him. Then it encom-
passed the trees themselves. One tree and then another, out-
ward in a widening circle of trees. Then everything under all
the trees, in the trees, everything that rubbed up against the
trees to make its mark, everything that grew around the trees
and because of the trees or even despite the trees. The whole
forest itself.

That is how he came to know that a flock of restless, name-
less souls was closing in on him. He could see it all from above.

III

John bent down to the water and cupped his dirty hands in it. He drank. A twig broke behind him, but John kept drinking.

Look at you, you common animal.

He did not have to turn around to know who, what, it was. Water dribbled from his soiled chin and he did not bother to wipe it. He tasted a faint residue of sweat and cosmetics, the metal taste of blood. He stayed in his crouch by the stream for a long time. When he stood and turned to face whatever it was, he faced nothing but the rustling leaves.

IV

The thing stalking him was something different altogether. It was itself some kind of animal. Something much too large for him to kill. When he circled back to see its tracks, he could fit both his feet inside one long, clawed footprint. Something so large and quiet could take him when it pleased. So he kept on.

Something was wrong with his stomach, but he needed to eat. He was dizzy from hunger. Underneath the rocks near another stream he found a palm's worth of slow, soft invertebrate creatures. These he swallowed without chewing and then he slurped straight from the trickle of water. He walked a good distance away from the stream and squatted behind a tree where he discharged a rank green liquid punctuated by dark viscous clumps. His insides cramped, and he could not walk. He crawled away from there to escape the smell, but some of it had splashed on the back of his legs. He lay on his side, a fallen S-curve, and slipped into and out of consciousness.

Sneaky little shit done shit himself. Who's so pretty now?

Then, as soon as the menacing voices started, they stopped. Like schoolboys caught by the teacher at recess. There was a heavy stillness common to the natural world, the time and space before a clash. Something large uttered a low growl. A loud rush of movement, the flurry of pursuit and evasion. Not voices anymore but shouts and screams, something caught on the dead run. The sounds of a massive predatory animal tearing another thing apart. And then again the heavy stillness. And then the large footfalls closed in on him. John clenched up. He could not run and, in the end, he did not want to. He felt the thing stand over him. He opened his eyes and was smacked in the face by a shaft of sunlight. The black figure moved to one side, shielding John's eyes from the light. For a fleeting moment, he stared straight into his dead father's smiling good eye. And then, just as quickly, it was another face. Whole and warm and lined.

"It's a good thing I'm only a little bit scared of haints," said Mose. "Lord if you sure don't got the looks of one."

V

It was slow going, getting John up from the ground and headed in the direction of Mose's small hermitage. John leaned on the old man, and they settled into a three-legged rhythm of steps. Mose steered them around the thick spots. When they needed to rest, they rested. There was the smell of old wood smoke. Somewhere off in the distance, a logging truck groaned. The State Road was not too far away. The land of the living. They limped up to the back of Mose's property. In the middle of the clearing was a humble wooden structure surrounded by a junkyard sculpture garden. Discarded auto parts, chains, truck tires, anvils, horseshoes, old green and brown glass bottles. A narrow dirt road led off in the direction of the State Road, but there was no working vehicle in sight.

Mose led John around to the side of the house, where he sat him on a stool made of a cut-off tree stump. He left him there, slumped and worn out from the walk. When he returned, he had a bucket of cool water and a sponge and a cake of brown lye soap. He also had an old-style straight edge razor; John's hair was an unsalvageable nest of mats and knots that would never get clean. John felt the hair fall around him in foul clumps.

When Mose had finished cropping the worst of the mats from John's hair, he helped him stand again and, without a word, he pulled the soiled dress over John's head. John swayed, and when the dress was off, Mose helped him sit back down on the stump. Then he dipped the sponge in the water and soaped it up thick. He washed John, every inch of him, filling bucket after bucket with the cool water to rinse him clean.

VI

Mose cut two thick slices from a slab of bologna. He readied a hotplate and fried the meat in a pan. The smell filled the house's one room.

John sat at a two-seat table wearing a clean but threadbare pair of workman's pants, two sizes two big. Mose had threaded a cord rope through the belt loops and tied it off at the front to keep them from falling down. John wore an old linen blazer and nothing else on top. His ruined feet were bare. Mose had washed them with great care and then applied an admixture of marigold petals and petroleum jelly that he had boiled down to make a salve.

John eyed the mattress on the floor, on the other side of the room. A small black and white television sat perched on a spindly stand at its foot. Everywhere else there were paintings, some still wet. The same apocalyptic paintings from the bar. Mose brought John a plate of sandwiches and a bottle of ketchup. The smell of food made John's stomach turn and it showed on his face.

"Might not be what you want," said the old man. "It's what I got." He went back to tidy up the cooking area. He returned to sit across the table from John, who picked at a corner of the white bread.

"You in a way," said Mose.

John nodded. Mose pointed to the paintings he had made.

"I been in a way for a long time now. That's how come I got all this up on the walls. I bet sometimes, if you like me, you get the feeling something's about to happen."

"Yes, sir," said John. His voice was thin and tremulous. "I do get that feeling."

"I had a notion something hurt and scared was headed out here," said Mose. "Hard to know about these feelings you get. How I see it, ain't a person left who ain't hurt and scared, so that coulda been anybody. But then I found you. In the state you was in. So then I knew it weren't just anybody headed out here. I knew it was you."

Mose rose and went to his easel. He returned with a small canvas, still wet. He handed the painting to John. A black and red buzzard flying into a dark blue night sky. Pinprick stars, a crescent moon. Flames reaching up from the bottom of the picture. The bird clutching a white garment with a red-brown stain dripping down the front of it. Screaming faces in the fire.

"I only paint what I see," said Mose. "This one come in my sleep, not long ago. Keep me up all night every night since. You hear what this one say?"

John shook his head, still lost in the picture he held in his hands.

"The world ain't long for this world," said Mose. "Never was supposed to be."

VII

John slept for all of one day and part of another. The old black man had gone about his business in the meantime, though he did not wander as far afield as was his wont, and he came back at regular intervals to check on his convalescing guest. When John woke, his mouth and throat were dry as stone. Mose was there, scratching at a canvas with a paint knife. He heard John stir and did not have to ask. He brought him a full mug of cool water.

"Sip," he said. "Too much at once ain't no good."

John sat up on the mattress and drank.

"You up just in time," said Mose. He had gone back to his work. "Man coming today, look at some pictures I got for sale."

John was still dizzy but he felt stronger. He tried to imagine the places he could hide. Under the house, maybe. Maybe he would have to venture back out into the woods. The road seemed too much of a risk.

"You ain't got to decide this second," said Mose. "But you want to be thinking on how things turn out from here."

"I don't want to see anybody," said John.

Mose kept up his knife work. He loaded it with a thick roll of paint, smeared it into the canvas with the flat.

"Things happening out there," said Mose. "You not the only one in a way about all this. That young lady you been running with got bad happenings up ahead."

"I know."

"Figured you might."

"She didn't do what they think she did," said John.

"You know that," said Mose, "and I know that. But the law don't know that. Law's a blunt tool for telling right from wrong."

Mose put down his palette and his knife.

"You better eat something," he said. "One way or other, you need your strength."

VIII

The days that he drove out to see Mose were, to the Man, both nervous and bright. Nervous because he knew how high his expectations were. They had grown to be impossible. He expected to lose his breath at the new work. He expected a vernacular transcendence. He expected to confront a gap, a wide one, between what he could say about the piece and what he knew it could mean.

He reached the turn off the State Road. There was no way to turn around once he had descended the driveway to Mose's house, so he had to do it here. He crossed the double yellow lines and drove onto the opposite shoulder, a little bit past the turn. Then he inched backwards, across both lanes and down the long, narrow dirt drive. It was downhill, and the loose dirt and gravel made for a series of stops, starts, and loudly spun wheels. There was worthwhile danger in all of it. Mose knew these sounds well.

"That's him now," he said.

John sat at the table finishing the last bite of a sandwich. He wiped his mouth with his hand. At the slight squeal of the van's brakes, Mose headed for the door.

"I'm fittin to meet my guest out here on the porch," he said. "Maybe you in here when we get back, maybe you aint. Long as you know they's only one way you gone get out of the mess you in. Sooner, later. Don't make no difference to me."

Mose opened the door just enough for himself to fit through and he shut it firm behind him. John heard the men greet one another, their footfalls on the porch. He did not take his eyes off the window, the world of trees, the blank green world it opened into.

The Man had loaded all the new paintings into the back of the van. He closed the double doors and went to Mose on the porch. The Man wore a look of worry on his face.

"I know what you thinking," said Mose. "Answer's still no. Not for double that."

"It's a fair offer," said the Man. "More than fair."

"Yes, sir, and you always been good to me. Good and fair."

"But no one ever said the art world was fair," the Man said.

"World-world neither. I won't sell the one you want. It ain't ready now. Might be never."

"I'll leave you be, then. Let you go paint some more pictures for me," said the Man. "All I ask is you make them the kind I can buy."

Mose raised his hand. "I do what I can do," he said.

Lost in disappointment, the Man opened the door to the van.

"I guess you're headed back into town then," said John. He sat in the passenger seat, the blood-stained dress balled in his lap. The Man stopped dead, his mouth just parted until it broke into a vague grimace.

"I'd ask," he said. "But I suspect I don't want to know."

"Yes," said John. He didn't look at him. "You don't."

"I told you to run," said the Man.

"You thought I'd be dead by now," said John. "And here I am."

The Man climbed into his seat and slammed the door. The young man in the passenger seat was leaner than he had been before, the line of his jaw somewhat more square. Without another word, the Man put the van in gear and eased it forward. Soon it ascended the hill up out of the woods, back onto the main road into town. A cargo of several dozen depictions of the Apocalypse.

IX

Mose went straight to his easel. He pulled out his palette, squeezed a dab of pure white from a tube. He loaded a brush thick with it and dabbed at the red-brown blotch.

X

A plain, thick woman in a uniform manned the receiving station at the county jail, her head buried in an automobile trader and a can of RC Cola at her fingertips. She adjusted her sidearm, sighed, and flipped the page. Someone approached the desk but she did not stir. A garment, soiled and brown and stained, dropped on her magazine. With instinctive disgust, she pushed back in her roller chair. Then her eyes found the young man who had dropped it there. His blue eyes, his hair that was choppy and uneven. Bruises on his face and neck. A patchy growth of stubble on his square jaw. And still, somehow, something soft and innocent in the way it all arrayed itself.

"I'm the one that killed Karl Adams," he said. "The stains are mostly him."

Covenant

I will be no cool cemetery vapor at your neck. I will wash you in warmth when you least expect it. That is just the kind of ghost I aim to be.

In the Beginning

I

A fist rapped on the door to the trailer. After a long while of nothing—no sound or sign of life within the house—there came a simple shuffling on the other side of the door, and it opened. Momma stood with her hand still on the knob. A man in a dark gray suit stood tentative before her. Right away, Momma was afraid of what he had to say. Not because he was tentative or previously unknown to her or even because he was unusually clean-cut and well-fed—he was all of these things—but because it was clear he was privy to a secret. Momma did not like secrets.

"Mrs. Ida Ray Temple?" he asked.

"Yes," she said, in a voice softer, sweeter than even she remembered. It had been so long since she or anyone had heard it last.

The man attempted a smile of assurance but was largely unsuccessful.

"I represent the estate of Mr. Joshua Merriwether," he said.

Momma stared at him with no expression. He frowned but he kept on.

"Took a while to track you down. You knew Mr. Merriwether?"

Momma shook her head no and went to shut the door.

"Your name meant something to him, Mrs. Temple," said the man, reaching out on a reflex to put his hand on the door. "He lived out in Uma growing up, just like you did."

Momma stopped.

"Mr. Merriwether was a private man. A reserved man. That made him a man of regrets. He remembered you. Even when you married and left town for good."

The man smiled at her. She did not return this nicety.

"Mr. Merriwether passed not long ago, ma'am. You may have heard about it on the news. It was a sensational circumstance."

She nodded.

"This is good news," he assured her. "Joshua Merriwether of Maycomb County has left you a considerable amount of money. Plus some land. And a trailer. Just about everything he had."

Momma braced herself against the door.

"It's true what they say about the mysterious ways of the Lord, isn't it, ma'am? You never know who's smiling with good favor upon you. Or for how long. Or from how far away."

Then Momma's eyes rolled into the back of her head and she fell out upon the floor.

II

Virginia stood straddling the tub, her broken foot outside of it, the rest of her underneath the warm stream of water. It was her first shower since she had been released. She felt a turning in her stomach and pushed past the plastic curtain. Before her bare knees hit the ground, what was in her gut spilled forth, bright and warm, into the commode.

III

In his room, Billy Ray was immersed in the business of trans-
forming himself. He had begun the painful process of committing large chunks of scripture to memory. With his injuries,
that meant searing headaches and sometimes seeing double.
This day he stood in front of the mirror, itself an act penance
due to the electric pain that shot down his weak legs, and he
recited the words of the Apostle Paul in his second letter to the
Corinthians:

> And lest I should be exalted above measure through the abundance of the
> revelations, there was given to me a thorn in the flesh, the messenger of
> Satan to buffet me, lest I should be exalted above measure. For this thing I
> besought the Lord thrice, that it might depart from me. And he said unto me,
> My grace is sufficient for thee: for my strength is made perfect in weakness.
> Most gladly therefore will I rather glory in my infirmities, that the power
> of Christ may rest upon me. Therefore I take pleasure in infirmities, in
> reproaches, in necessities, in persecutions, in distresses for Christ's sake: for
> when I am weak, then am I strong.

And then came the great thump of his mother at the threshold.
He strained his ear for something that would explain the
noise, but there was nothing else to hear. After a moment, he
found the cane that kept him steady in his ventures outside
the room, and Billy Ray labored down the hallway to see about
what had made such an ominous sound. He shuffled into the
living room, where a strange man in a gray suit made a feeble
attempt to fan his mother back into consciousness. She stirred
some and moaned.

"God Almighty," Billy Ray said to the man at the door.
"What the Sam Hill you trying to sell us?"

IV

Not far from there, another kind of search and surfacing got underway. Broad-chested men donned scuba gear. They went in the gray morning when it was somewhat cooler and the bottom of the lake was more likely to be calm. They had divided the body of water into roughly equivalent sections, and the six frogmen would scour the bottom one section at a time. A sunken corpse can be capricious. It has no motive to reveal itself. Knowing what they faced, they made a competition of it. A case of beer to the one who dredged it up. Another to the one who guessed the right section of the lake. The hours were slow. Morning threatened to become midday, then the impossibly hot afternoon. But then a diver emerged, the others still crawling along the bottom, inch by inch, unaware. He lifted his mask and shouted out to the crew on shore. They, in turn, came to a quick and merry realization. The same man had won both cases of beer. The winner of this embarrassment of riches pulled the bloated body in tow, just beneath the surface of the water. It bobbed up, ravaged but also cleansed, ready to meet its final dispensation on the earth.

V

Chewie put his foot to the shoulder of a spade. It penetrated the firm, ancient earth. The nights were getting cooler, and he felt good to be out in it. He dug until his hands were warm in the places of friction with the handle. Soon the sharp edge of the spade pierced a plastic bulge. He unearthed the precious lode and brought to the river bank. He walked with it out into the middle of the current. One by one, he pulled the individual baggies from the larger sack as it floated on the surface. One by one, he opened the individual packages and spilled all they held into the river.

IV

The Father and the Son

I

Now he found himself at a long table. A fluorescent glow above him. He scribbled a few more words in the last available space of a composition book, then he put the stubby No. 2 down. He enclosed the book and four others just like it in a large manila envelope and sealed it up. His own final dispensation to send out into the world. Search and surface.

Soon enough, he would inhabit a gray-white room, windowless, empty except for the plain gurney onto which he was to be strapped. The technician, a man with graying hair and a mustache, would remove John's glasses. Two other men would waste no time or motion in strapping him down and then stand at attention. The technician would tie the rubber tubing around the right arm and find a vein, swab it, then do the same with the left and insert the IVs. The saline drip would begin, and then the man would attach the heart monitor. Then John would close his eyes, an adjacent room of empty chairs bearing witness to all of it from behind a pane of darkened glass.

———

A trinity of separate injections. Sodium thiopental. Pancuronium bromide. Potassium chloride. Harsh chemicals. The first renders the prisoner unconscious. The second induces paralysis. The third stops the heart. The whole thing takes seven minutes. Some believe there is the sensation of drowning.

II

A slim boy ran out of the large house into the bright afternoon and down the long drive to the mailbox. He was at the cusp of adolescence, his features still fine and faintly childish. Long-ish hair. He pulled all the mail out and looked at each piece. There was a large package. To his surprise, it was addressed to him:

CHRISTIAN TEMPLE
205 LAKECREST WAY
E—, AL 35405

Christian brought the mail into the house and dropped it on a table next to the door. He kept the large envelope and took it with him to the couch to open it. His mother walked into the room, a calm and old black dog in her arms. Virginia was somehow prettier for the slight crow's feet, the fifteen pounds she had never lost after Christian's birth.

"Young man. I thought I told you to get ready for church this evening. It's Wednesday."

"I hate going to church on Wednesday," said Christian. "Sunday's enough."

"I think you wouldn't talk so tough if your daddy was around," she said. "What has gotten into you lately? You know how upset he gets if we aren't front row center and right on time for the sermon. If you look nice, maybe we'll be on camera like last time. You want to be on the camera, don't you?"

Christian ignored her and pulled out the composition books, tossing the envelope on the floor.

"I swear not a person in this house listens to a word I say. *That* you get from your daddy."

She tried to make out what her son was holding, but she could not see what it was, so she walked over to him to get a closer look.

"What have you got? And how much do you want to bet me it's something you're not supposed to have?"

"Mail," said the boy, without looking up. He had opened one of the books and started flipping through the pages. "For me. Daddy says gambling is—"

"A gateway to darker things," said Virginia. "I know that's what he says. Your daddy says a lot of things."

She bent down and picked the envelope up off the floor. When she read the return address, she put Edward down on and sat on the couch next to the boy.

"Hand that book over right now. I need to see what it says."

Christian protested but she grabbed it from him and read. Soon she was turning pages, not so much reading them but taking them in, touching them with a reverence reserved for what they were: evidence of a former life, another time and place, another version of herself. Not unlike the boy next to her. She ran her fingers over the indentations the words made in the paper. There was writing in block letters and cursive, there were drawings and pasted-in parts. Dispatches from some distant place. She closed the book before she succumbed to the temptation to bring it to her face in a gesture of tenderness. Instead she kissed Christian's forehead and handed the book back to him, then she scooped Edward up and climbed the stairs to get dressed for church.

III

Christian ran as if he was late for something. He bolted down the street of his gated subdivision clutching one of the books. The asphalt was smooth and black, and each square, green lawn was a testament to the plain geometry of the rational human mind. He passed the stately houses, the mammoth community swimming pool, the championship golf course trimmed just so. The places where he had marked the important moments of his inconsequential life: birthday parties, Little League banquets, sleepovers, assorted holidays. The limited sum total of his world to date. And now there was a book to hold tight in the crook of his arm. A parcel from nowhere. Or at least from somewhere else.

When he came to the outer gate at the State Road, he scampered across it and ducked through a shortcut in the woods. His lungs ached. He pressed on through the trees and leaves and brush, until it all opened up into a wide, clear space that shimmered with the reflection of a setting sun. A hawk skimmed the surface of the lake. Christian, breathing hard, sat by the water, near the lookout point, and opened the book for the first of what would become many times.

The First and Last Apocalypse of John the Revelator—

A Book of Limited Wisdom and Unsolicited Admonitions, Collected from Various Sources, as Addressed to the One Who Will Come After Him.

> All things are delivered unto me of my Father: and no man knoweth the Son, but the Father; neither knoweth any man the Father, save the Son, and he to whomsoever the Son will reveal him.
> —*Matthew 11:27*

You want an explanation of how you came to be. There is also the plain truth that none of us ever gets this explanation. Not all-of-it. Not in a sequence anyone can understand.

A word about recollection. What you want to remember and what you do remember is nearly never the same thing. The stories and lies are bridges.

———

A fetus in the womb is more fish than hominid. Its tiny lungs suck liquid and its eyes are of little use. What it mainly does is swim and swim in its dim and cozy habitat. Then the world ends: it is plucked out, into another universe altogether. The rules have changed. The elements are wholly different, mixed up, catawampus:

The light is brutal bright;

That which was abundant before is now scarce;

What was compact is now infinite.

Worse, the infant itself is something else too: it makes a noise, it sees that it's a part of the awful world around it. In the moment of truth, either it becomes this new thing, breathes the air and kicks its legs, or that is the end of that.

———

Womb

—*noun*

1. The belly; the abdomen. [Obs.] *Chaucer.*

And he coveted to fill his **woman** of the cods that the hogs eat, and no man gave him. *Wyclif (Luke xv. 16).*
An I had but a belly of any indifferency, I were simply the most active fellow in Europe. My **womb**, my **womb**, my **womb** undoes me. *Shak.*

2. (Anat.) The uterus. See Uterus.

3. The place where anything is generated or produced.

The **womb** of earth the genial seed receives. *Dryden.*

4. Any cavity containing and enveloping anything.

The center spike of gold Which burns deep in the bluebell's **womb**. *R. Browning.*

———

All of us were born kicking and fighting to live. But we have become used to the soft life. We have become creatures of comfort. We dislike inconveniences and discomforts. So, what happens when we are faced with a survival situation with its stresses, inconveniences, and discomforts? This is when the will to live—placing a high value on living—is vital. The experience and knowledge you have gained through life and through your Army training have bearing on your will to live. Stubbornness, a refusal to give in to problems and obstacles that face you, will give you the mental and physical strength to endure.
—*The U.S. Army Survival Manual.*

———

Man alone at the very moment of his birth, cast naked upon the naked earth, does she abandon to cries and lamentations.
—Pliny the Elder, *Natural History.*

———

A boy is, of all wild beasts, the most difficult to manage.
—Plato.

———

A riddle:

> *1) When I was a child, the world was simple.*
> *2) I was never a child.*

The Truth is somewhere in between.

———

The fewer the words, the better the prayer.
—Martin Luther.

———

This is what there is to learn from the woods Listen to the quiet it makes. There is unrelenting malice in it. Or a lack of sentiment, which is the same thing close enough. Yes it makes a sound when you are not there and when you are. Just the same. It makes no difference. This is no philosophy. Or majesty. Or magic. God does not whisper the way the trees whisper. Like you are not even there. Like you are nothing but a cooling corpse. Which is just exactly what you are.

———

Two of the gravest general dangers to survival are the desire for comfort and a passive outlook.
—*The U.S. Army Survival Manual.*

———

Winter months do move the slowest. Bone chills and wet rains. The current age, such as it is, is one long series of winter month after winter month. A low, gray sky. Vapored breath. One night not long ago I dreamed it rained like a son of a bitch. I mean it was a cold and cleansing sort of downpour. A deluge. All the trees were heavy and black and the little hut I lived in proved itself a porous shelter. It was no mind to me as I stripped down to my slick birthday suit and played out in it. So as to be efficient, I brought out a pan of dried beans that would catch a covering of fresh rainwater in which to soak. I played and played and was a muddy cuss, twigs in my hair. It did not matter to me one bit because I knew the rain would never stop, not for a good long time anyway, and there would be ample opportunity to rinse off the black world. When that time came and I was clean again and breathless, I knew I could lie prone on the floor of my hut and think about how lucky I was to know exactly what my life would amount to. How I knew that later on there would be some singing monks on the Educational TV, that I would listen to them in the dark and the rain and be halfway convinced that the world was at heart a peaceful, sacred place. How the next day I would simmer up those soaked beans along with maybe a couple of beautiful strips of pig fat and plenty of salt and then, after several bowls of it, I would crouch on a three-foot stump deep in the woods and squeeze out a black plug, long and straight, from my coiling insides. This is the manner in which a man becomes straight and pure again. Yes, I said to myself in my dream, I am so lucky to know what will become of me. I know you think you are not so lucky. You think you know not when the winter will end. That the best you can hope for is to turn away from the whole mess of wintry indeterminates and seek some transient kind of warmth and light, a picture you can bear to look at. If you knew what I know, it would all be different. That is why I will come clean. What is a seer who cannot share his vision? Here it is boiled down: Yes. Something Else is coming. And yes that Something Else is you.

———

But make no mistake: the world is not waiting. It gave up on the likes of you a long time ago. Rest assured you're on your own now, to do as you please.

———

Being isolated under trying and threatening conditions
will often bring on another stress—a feeling of
loneliness—which can lead to feelings of helplessness and
despair. Self-sufficiency plays a major role in overcoming
these feelings.
—*The U.S. Army Survival Manual.*

———

You will have occasion to ask why you should listen to me. I am thinking of the way an older man tells a younger man who is better than him—stronger, smarter, more handsome—what he should do with a woman. The younger man will find himself in positions the older man has never imagined. But the older man tells him all he knows anyway, asks him does he know where this or that delicate treasure hides itself, and that you should be gentle with it but sometimes not too gentle. And so on. It has nothing to do with the younger man. It is because the older man has never known the truth of what he is saying until he says it. It is because the older man cannot understand himself until he tells the younger man everything he has ever known or done. What he's seen and what he wishes he'd seen. The true parts and the lies. He is not living it again. He never lived it. It did not exist until he told about it. Ask me who your father is and I will tell you it is not any one man at all. All of your fathers have failed you. All of your fathers were weaker, dumber, less handsome than you. There is nothing we could have told you that you did not already know. It is not for you that I am telling you. None of this was ever for you. You were always going to come into being just as you are in any event. Thank heavens. Amen.

———

You can increase your self-sufficiency—your ability to function competently on your own—with practice. You have opportunities to do so each day of your life: Make your own decisions and rely on yourself; explore new situations and solve problems. You must learn to accept the reality of a new situation or of an emergency and then take suitable action. This is one of the most important psychological requirements for survival.
—*The U.S. Army Survival Manual.*

———

Do well and right and let the world sink.
—Herbert, *Country Parson*.

———

By now I hope you know that we are lost for good and you can't save us. By now I hope you know that even you will get old and your lungs will take less air and then less air and then less air until all of the rest of you is too tired to leave the warm, stale bed. Your stomach will not hold anything. Its foul air will swirl around you. Sphincters loosened all the way up and down the interlocked canals of your insides. All manner of humors spilling out of you. That is a human thing and it will happen to you as it happens to all of us. I am not prophesying the end of all days. I do not believe in that. I am only prophesying the end of your days. There is a difference.

———

Humor

—*noun*

1. Moisture, especially, the moisture or fluid of animal bodies, as the chyle, lymph, etc.; as, the humors of the eye, etc. &hand; *The ancient physicians believed that there were four humors (the blood, phlegm, yellow bile or choler, and black bile or melancholy), on the relative proportion of which the temperament and health depended.*

2. (Med.) A vitiated or morbid animal fluid, such as often causes an eruption on the skin. A body full of *humors.*" *Sir W. Temple.*

3. State of mind, whether habitual or temporary (as formerly supposed to depend on the character or combination of the fluids of the body); disposition; temper; mood; as, good humor; ill humor.

Examine how your **humor** is inclined, And which the ruling passion of your mind. *Roscommon.*
A prince of a pleasant **humor**. *Bacon.*
I like not the **humor** of lying. *Shak.*

4. pl. Changing and uncertain states of mind; caprices; freaks; vagaries; whims.

Is my friend all perfection, all virtue and discretion? Has he not **humors** to be endured? *South.*

5. That quality of the imagination which gives to ideas an incongruous or fantastic turn, and tends to excite laughter or mirth by ludicrous images or representations; a playful fancy; facetiousness.

For thy sake I admit That a Scot may have **humor**, I'd almost said wit. *Goldsmith.*
A great deal of excellent **humor** was expended on the perplexities of mine host. *W. Irving.*
Aqueous humor, Crystalline humor ∨ lens, Vitreous humor. (Anat.) See Eye. — Out of humor, dissatisfied; displeased; in an unpleasant frame of mind. Syn. — Wit; satire; pleasantry; temper; disposition; mood; frame; whim; fancy; caprice. See Wit.

———

This from the Psalms:

Then the earth shook and trembled;
the foundations also of the hills moved and were shaken,
because he was wroth.
There went up smoke out of his nostrils,
and fire out of his mouth devoured:
coals were kindled by it.
He bowed the heavens also, and came down:
and darkness was under his feet.
And he rode upon a cherub, and did fly:
yea, he did fly upon the wings of the wind.
He made darkness his secret place:
his pavilion round about him were dark waters
and thick clouds of the skies.
At the brightness that was before him his thick clouds
    passed,
hail stones and coals of fire.
The LORD also thundered in the heavens,
and the Highest gave his voice;
hail stones and coals of fire.
Yea, he sent out his arrows, and scattered them;
And he shot out lightnings, and discomfited them.
Then the channels of waters were seen,
and the foundations of the world were discovered:
at thy rebuke O LORD,
at the blast of thy nostrils.

He sent from above, he took me,
he drew me out of many waters.
He delivered me from my strong enemy,
and from them which hated me:
for they were too strong for me.
They prevented me in the day of my calamity:
but the LORD was my stay.
He brought me forth also into a large place:
he delivered me, because he delighted in me.

And:

The LORD rewarded me according to my righteousness,
    according to the cleanness of my hands hath he rec-
    ompensed me.

But then there is the Shelton woman who I almost forgot until this very moment. Who lived alone out on a sick and fallow farm near where I was raised. Whose house was big and empty but for the fat brazen rats. Who had always had nothing. Who must not have ever felt full of anything that could sustain her. Whose husband had succumbed to wasting disease and left her to the slow silence of her own mind. Who, in turn, counted him the lucky one. Who could not remember a time—not even as a child—when she did not wish the end of days upon herself. Who started in the night from the sound of it coming at her and to her. Yes like a locomotive. Like an angry god in the shape and sound of a long steel train. Yes it plucked her up from her very filthy old-woman bed. Yes it pulled her straight up where the roof used to be. Yes she somersaulted a quarter-mile through the air and yes it impaled her on the thick black limb of a long dead tree. It took her that way. According to the cleanness of her hands. According to her justice.

———

Wisdom is what the world cuts off you. The particulars do not matter in the end. Whether you are slung up in a tree by meteorological cataclysm. Whether you are hunted by an assassin. Whether you are anyone, ever, anywhere. My request is that in the numbered days you have left you do not suggest otherwise in either your words or deeds. That would make you a simple merchandiser. I was wrong about everything else—yes, whatever I thought I knew is not what I have come to find out—but I know I am right about this. Solace and comfort never saved a thing. Salvation is a piercing siren call. Salvation is a thing that smarts. Or if not salvation—maybe it was always too late for that, for me—then just a matter of being brave and wakeful.

———

Old men are fond of giving good advice, to console themselves for being no longer in a position to give bad examples.
—La Rochefoucauld.

I am not old but my bones do creak. Bodies unhinge. I feel my heartbeat in my throat. It is not growing fainter. It is the opposite of faint. It is a thud too desperate in its efforts to be heard. I do not sleep through the night. Some say in days to come there will be a lake of fire to transform the damned into the hot dust of a desert. The truest definition of Hell. Nothing left to remember them by. And a demon is the one who cannot wait for that to come.

Color me, then, a demon.

———

As we advance in life, we learn the limits of our abilities.
—Froude, *Short Studies on Great Subjects*.

———

Am I making you sad? There is nothing sad about any of it. There are no tragedies or comedies. Only the one single way it has been for all of us, always. There is no such thing as why or how or once upon a time. Only what is right there in front of you. In the present tense. As awful and gorgeous as it is.

———

And anyway: you are a big boy, advancing in life.

———

I do remember one thing from when I myself was a boy. I was a swimming fish, the water warm as a living human body. I grew whiskers. They were how I found my way. I did not need my eyes. The pond was deep and on the bottom the water got cooler. Down there, I could taste the mud. The others gathered around me. Who are you—where did you come from? No. Fish don't ask questions. They go to the new thing and bump up against it to know what it is. Or they hide and don't concern themselves with knowing. I was like them. I was safe. We did what fish do. We swam in a school. We snapped at insects on the surface. Our bellies were never full enough. We slept and dreamed open-eyed dreams. I forgot that I had ever been something else. Above us in the oblivion there were stars and mountains. Things smiled, they flew, they dug into the ground. I was happy and unconcerned with any of it. All a fish can do is swim.

And that, young man, is as close to the truth of it as any of us can ever get.

Rapture

Something of the former young prophet stands tentative in a room, a place not unlike a gray-white execution chamber. Except here there is a small window. A portal back into and out of the world. The empty prison yard yawns below. A buzzard circles over it. A body—what was his body—still strapped to the plain gurney. A gray haired, mustachioed executioner checks his watch, probes the dead wrist for a pulse. He checks and rechecks the heart monitor, then he marks the time for the official record. The bird sweeps once more over the empty yard and starts a slow, steady advance upon the setting sun.

Elsewhere. Another time and place. A hawk skims the surface of a manmade lake. The bird plucks a slick fish from the water and climbs higher and higher into the afternoon sky. The fish wriggles once and then again and then is calm. A boy closes a book and watches the bird disappear into a warm, retreating sun. All of it washed in perfect orange light. Everything peaceful and serene. As close to the truth as we can ever get.

TJ Beitelman teaches creative writing at the
Alabama School of Fine Arts in Birmingham.
He can be found on-line at www.tjbman.com
and at www.try101.org. For more about John
the Revelator, please visit www.facebook.com/
johntherevelatorbook.